SPY DOCTORS AND THE ARAB SPRING

BY

MIKE LAUNER

 New Generation **Publishing**

1

Diogenes was lying on his stained camp bed in a dingy inner-city apartment. The air conditioning was straining to function and the atmosphere was clogged with diesel fumes. He flicked an insect at the wall in a version of kamikaze cockroach and wandered over to the window. He shook his head and fastened his scruffy jeans and splashed his face with lukewarm water from the tap on the wall, and used his free hand to search for his cigarettes in the drawer. Through dripping fingers he saw that the Camel packet was empty; when he glanced at the rickety table he also saw that the whisky bottle had run dry. This was serious. Unless he had an immediate infusion of alcohol and tobacco he would end up like his father. From under the bed he pulled out his tobacco box and rummaged through his bundle of passports. He slipped one into the back pocket of his jeans and pulled a few notes from under the bed.

The stairwell was dark and had, for some years, functioned as a refuse deposit. Diogenes kicked the heavy stuff out of his way as he made his way to the outer door which was open and led to a square where some plied their trade whilst others tried to relieve passing visitors of valuables. He headed towards the shop, avoiding the mess and discarded cigarettes, and he pushed his way through the locals. The men wore old jackets and worn overalls, the women had traditional dresses designed to hide their bodies from other men. Their husbands had taken good money for them, to relieve fathers of the burden. Sometimes he yearned for parents and had a feeling of resentment when he saw families together. Why couldn't he have had a family?

He pointed to the Camel brand and picked out a

bottle of counterfeit whisky as he passed over a few notes. The proprietor loved customers like him; in, cash, and then out, with none of the babble in between. He pushed his way back to his room, pausing to relieve himself behind a wall next to the butchers. As he unlocked his door he heard a ring tone. He pulled out another box from under the bed, where he rummaged through a collection of mobile phones. One was flashing and he fished it out and pressed the green button.

'Yes,' he said, 'Diogenes speaking.'

'When?'

'So I've got half an hour to get to the airport?'

'OK, I'll pick them up.' Diogenes cut off the call.

He selected two passports and bundled some money into his pocket, then sprinted down the stairwell, unlocked a moped from the lamppost and set off at some speed. It was congested with ancient vehicles. Some had been abandoned; others had the driver tinkering under the bonnet. Lorries were overflowing and unbalanced, and tended to spill their load at regular intervals which produced heaps of anything from scrap iron to dead chickens. Everyone smoked and the central reservations seemed to be a home for prostitutes plying their wares amid the fog, gas fumes and humidity. Moped was the transport of choice here and, within his half-hour deadline, Diogenes was at the ticket counter. He used his height and his fierce blue eyes to force his way to the front. At the departure gate he explained that he had lost his luggage, which didn't stop him being pulled aside by the security staff. He made it clear that he could not understand any of their languages and that he was carrying nothing except money and a passport. The last one on the plane, he was plied with drink and titbits. He checked his ticket, which was marked business class, destination Geneva.

Diogenes didn't usually eat much, especially when food had been selected for him, which seemed to make the over-attentive stewardesses concerned for his welfare. He was embarrassed when people offered him food; he wasn't used to feeling included. On the other hand he was happy with free whisky and a bar snack. This was an approximation of his regular daily diet and it was only the no smoking sign that concerned him. After they had landed at the airport he watched the passengers fighting to disembark and smiled. Diogenes tended to smile a lot at his fellows, especially at their concerns with possessions and families. He had to, otherwise he would weep and, in his line of business, to show weakness could be fatal. Finally he slunk down the embarkation tunnel to supply his passport to another uniformed official pretending to be on the lookout for terrorists. Diogenes had met his fair share of these and knew that they didn't bother with security checks. As he moved towards the exit, he negotiated his way around elderly tourists with improbable luggage piled on trolleys that were out of control with their breathless navigators moving in a crab-like fashion across the corridor. He scanned the meeters and greeters for a version of his name. A fat man in a suit directed him towards an obligatory Mercedes in the car park across from the terminal. There was no conversation with the driver, who delivered him like a parcel to an office block overlooking Lake Geneva.

He was ushered to a room on the sixteenth floor that was vast and empty. He took a seat in a steel black leather chair at one end of a deserted wooden table. Before long a slim-suited man wearing rimless bifocals appeared holding a black carry-on suitcase.

'Do you know why we have brought you here?' Leonardo asked.

Diogenes shrugged, he had been here and other

similar places like it many times before. Indeed most of his life had been spent in large institutions.

'Here are your instructions,' said Leonardo. 'Everything is in the case, including a photograph. We are time-limited for the usual reasons and you are free to stay here in Geneva. The car will take you to your accommodation. Do you have any questions?'

Diogenes was certain that if he were to return there within half an hour there would be no trace of the meeting and even the most advanced forensic teams would draw a blank. The instructions led him to a car that took him into a five-star hotel where the room key opened a superior suite. Diogenes sat down on one of the two king-sized beds with his new suitcase, only rising to attend to his needs in the facilities. There was a Jacuzzi and a series of lights around the rim that he discovered would project multi-coloured images onto the ceilings in a mood-enhancing fashion. He estimated that the opulent vanity set alone would have a resale value that would cover the cost of a room in a lesser establishment. Opening the case, he discovered some clothes and a note about their disposal after use; his employers were not in the laundry business. There were several sealed envelopes that were date and time labelled, and a mobile phone with a list of numbers. He had seen this arrangement before and knew that any money would be moved electronically into one of his accounts. Not that he had much use for money; he'd never had any as a child, as his mother had spent what little there was on herself. Diogenes had grown up to believe that possessions would only be taken by others and pension provisions were there, if required. He immersed himself in the Jacuzzi à la lumière and selected some appropriate music from the menu. He had not checked out the lounge and dining room, having little use for either, but before long he had a visit from two naked girls who had been waiting to assist with the lavage and utilise the designer soaps and gels. After the tasks had been completed along with the après lavage, they silently dressed and left him in a comfortable position with their calling card. He slept well that night.

Diogenes had been awake for a while thinking about his programme when room service breakfast arrived. A meeting was scheduled at ten-thirty on the university campus with a scientist, followed by further meetings on the same campus.

His name was Professor Lockstein, and he was waiting in his office to welcome Diogenes with a coffee and some Swiss biscuits. Without ado he began to cover a whiteboard with Greek symbols and numbers and launched into his discussion. 'I assume you are aware of our position so far, sir'.

'Very much so, professor,' said Diogenes.

'That is good. I was hoping we wouldn't have to go through the preliminaries. So tiresome. Can I ask how you have become so well acquainted with our work?' asked Lockstein.

'I get emails and am well grounded in the area.'

'OK, so we are at the moment here,' said Lockstein, pointing at a Greek symbol, 'and we are hoping to be here, in a couple of months,' he said, pointing at another.

Diogenes nodded.

'Your people have indicated that you need to be at our level for your work. Is there anything here that I can help you with?'

'Yes, I am working with applied nanochemistry and I was looking into the trans-exchange of the information at level three. We are quite advanced in deciphering molecules for military hardware, whether they are bombs or other ordinance, but we need remote wireless systems so that we can change their viability. Can you see any contraindications to this?' asked Diogenes.

'I will have to check with the director, but I can't see that interdepartmental collaboration should be any great problem. On the contrary, this supports our assertion that the project has many different applications and helps with our funding,' said the professor.

Diogenes stood up, shook hands and walked down four blocks to the department of nanochemistry. Checking his envelopes, he found that en route he was due to visit a medical centre for blood tests that had been pre-arranged by his employers prior to one of his future assignments. His work took him to inhospitable areas and it was not just the physical risks of the places but also he had to be prepared for threats from the local population. After the doctors had finished bleeding him and sealing the bottles, he provided them with labels from an envelope, which contained coded information to tie in with his missions. He hailed a taxi to return him to his hotel and he found a key to the hotel gym where he started pounding the cross trainer until he was covered in pools of sweat. He had always been taught that a healthy mind required a healthy body, and apart from the single malt and the cigarettes he found that the balance of physical and mental exercise was best for him. Back in his room he opened the last envelope to reveal his flight ticket and new passport with a visa to St Petersburg.

He had been allocated business class again and this provided an opportunity for a sleep in between several whisky refills before the plane shuddered to a halt outside a large modified hangar that constituted St Petersburg airport. After disembarkation the passengers were herded into an immigration hall that had more officials than passengers. Diogenes could feel tightness around his temples as he was aware of being scrutinised, not only by the military, but more worryingly, by their colleagues in government-issue suits. The scrutiny of his new passport seemed to take forever as the diminutive bespectacled immigration clerk checked and rechecked it against a multitude of websites. Once released, Diogenes was quickly propelled outside, from where he saw that the airport was in reality just a jazzed up hangar, probably a relic from the war. A car was waiting for him and they soon became stuck in a traffic jam as a procession passed by, and the driver turned round and advised Diogenes that this could take some hours and it was probably best to walk to his hotel, which was just off the main road and the best one in town. Diogenes realised that he had been committed to tip the driver quite handsomely and as he found some roubles amongst the money in his envelope he started to count them out when the driver shook his head and said US dollars. Diogenes found some dollars and as he was counting them out the driver examined each note and appeared to reject the worn ones in favour of the crisp new ones. Diogenes got out as the driver smiled and pointed to the left of the street as Diogenes checked his envelope for the name of the hotel.

Diogenes was on Nevski Prospekt, a wide road which was packed with banks of old men in dirty overcoats, fur hats and some medals pinned onto the front. Some were carrying banners and there was music played by callow youths in cheap uniforms from cadet corps. It was difficult to walk down the street because of sheer numbers and many of them seemed to have survived the siege of Leningrad, and widows were also marching, proudly displaying their late husbands' medals. It brought back the fleeting memories of his father's RAF uniform stuffed under the wardrobe, untouched since he had been demobbed a year before Diogenes had been born.

The crowd had brought flasks of vodka and parcels of food wrapped in newspaper to protect them against the cold.

Diogenes was getting so cold that his ears seemed to be frozen to his head. Then he came across some black market traders set back from the street. A glass of vodka was offered and accepted.

'Hello, I am Alexei,' a trader announced. 'Can I offer you anything, perhaps Soviet militaria, genuine oil paintings or smart fur hats, Russian style, as worn in Arctic?'

Diogenes surveyed the mountains of goods on the stalls that seemed to be operated by Alexei's staff. He tried on a thick black busby-type hat.

'Twenty dollars US,' said Alexei.

He thought of the hat as a lifesaver rather than a fashion item and he was aware that he had been in danger of succumbing to frostbite. He knew that after his frozen ears the rest of his body and limbs would have soon followed suit.

'I have more goods in here and if you want from somebody else, I can arrange it cheap for you,' said Alexei.

Diogenes followed him into a block of flats and up some stairs, where whole families were huddled together amongst the grime and damp with a faulty gas fire full on. Diogenes was ushered into a large room full of military uniforms and equipment.

'You want the uniform of a full admiral, Soviet navy? Good price. Try it on, go on,' offered Alexie.

Diogenes reluctantly pulled on the jacket complete with medals and fastened the gold buttons. The sleeves came halfway up his arms and caused Diogenes and

Alexei to laugh like old friends.

'You want medals, I have them all here. This one is the highest in the land like the British Victoria cross. I can sell it to you if you buy the hat, for ten dollars US.'

Diogenes could see through the grimy window the old soldiers and their widows proudly marching down Nevski Prospekt, the grand old street planned by Peter the Great, and he sighed.

'And I have this one,' continued Alexei amongst the boxes of military bric-a-brac. 'A silver medal, real silver, for women for having ten children. The gold is for fifteen. I don't have any, but I can get some, I go to Moscow next week and meet my friend.'

Ten children, most of who would have joined the Red army and received more medals and worn ill-fitting suits; it was distressing.

'I have to leave before next week, so I will just take the hat,' said Diogenes.

'Where are you staying?'

'I don't know yet, I have just arrived,' lied Diogenes.

'Come on, you stay with me.'

There was a makeshift bed in the corner covered with chickens and Alexei cleared them off to reveal some eggs.

'Bed and breakfast!' he joked.

Diogenes did not like to enquire about the facilities in the building, but he guessed that it did not compare favourably with Geneva hotels. In the event he smiled and left before finding his posh hotel just off the Prospekt. The commissionaires were more like uniformed KGB as they studied him for any sign of mental weakness before allowing him through the metal detector into the lobby. The hotel was in the Old Russian tradition with marble floor and high ceilings. When the porter showed him into his room he found that even the floors were warm, and after he parted with a few more pristine dollars, he dived into the minibar and lay on the bed as he found a photograph in his envelope with a room number that was on the same floor. Although the photograph was a little faded he could make out some oriental features and an Arabic sounding name.

The next morning he was informed that his transport was there and a black Mercedes with darkened windows was waiting for him on the ice covered side street. He quickly had a wash and gathered his belongings and before long was in the airport having a shower in the business lounge. There were only a few business class passengers on the London Gatwick flight and as breakfast (with whisky) was served, he was given the first edition of the *Kommersant*, the Russian business morning paper. There was a picture of the man that had been in the photograph given to him in Geneva, with a caption underneath. The stewardess kindly translated.

"Diplomat found dead in his bed, no known cause".

2

When adult males dream it is usually about someone like Ingrid; tall, blonde, with a perfect body and her tan is real, like the rest of her. She had been a beauty queen, a model, an athlete, a grade-A student and married to a millionaire.

She was topping up her tan on the beach in Angleholm in the south-west of Sweden when her BlackBerry rang to remind her of an appointment. Gathering together her bikini top and a few other essentials, she jumped into her Porsche and drove to her apartment in Helsingborg. From there it was only a matter of about an hour to Copenhagen airport via the ferry boat at Helsingor, the home of Hamlet's castle and the giant who is said to reside in the dungeons. Like much in Scandinavia, it was difficult to separate fact from folklore, even down to the duty free shop, where alcohol was absent and chocolate proliferated. The rest was left to the gold credit card which avoided the need for cash for someone like Ingrid who needed kronor, euros and dollars, sometimes all in the same day. It helped if the card was corporate and available for first class travel to New York and then to Nashville, Tennessee. She arrived in New York Kennedy airport and the Homeland security in New York showed minimal interest in her papers as she waited to catch an American Eagle flight to Nashville with country music artists and their instruments. She was able to check-in, ready to freshen up and meet her old flame Chuck McNulty, complete with black Stetson and guitar case. There was something about country and western stars which reversed the old rule dictating that goodies wore white Stetsons and baddies wore black ones. In Herbie's steak bar, Chuck had ordered her favourite, medium rare buffalo, so tender and rich that you could understand why thousands of Amerindians had chosen to die rather than let the cavalry help themselves. Chuck opened the conversation; Ingrid was known by her country and western stage name of Sue Dakota.

'What y'all been up to, Sue?'

Chuck was a man of few words but his rockabilly style had won over most of the old Confederate states and all the music moguls. Ingrid washed the buffalo down with the traditional Budweiser and some good old Lynchburg Tennessee whisky. Chuck stuck to sarsaparilla due to some previous indiscretions. Ingrid had rhinestones which matched her eyes and a fawn suede outfit with the fringes a bit like a cross between Hiawatha and Davey Crocket.

The country music awards the following night brought out all the hats and the fake tan. But Ingrid seemed to have her name on most of the female awards before she was whisked off to perform at the Grand Old Opry. The show was split into parts broadcast live on national radio, with advertisements in between read out by an old pro who introduced each section. She was waiting in the wings when the oldest man in the world managed to lug his guitar behind his Zimmer frame and warm up the packed house with veterans and families. She did her bit, with every red neck in the hall whooping their lungs to bits. Chuck was waiting behind the stage tuning up his guitar and comparing his Stetson with the rest of the acts, but no-one could beat the old timer Hollerin' Hank on the Cajun concertina. Sue was about to take the stage amidst the flashing cameras and cell phones when the announcer, who was not one for understatement, described her as the finest country singer since Patsy Clyne. Her own introduction was drowned by whistles and whooping which only subsided when she led into the first bars of her hit single 'Country Love is Best'. Her second and final song was an old classic of hers concerning a bartender, which made Chuck wince a little, but was an essential part of his rehabilitation.

Back at the hotel Ingrid was eating her breakfast American style with a fork; she always thought that this must have developed when the settlers were on the range with no table or chairs, and a knife was used for removing buffalo hide or Sioux scalps. Eggs over easy with some hard bacon and grits along with oats for a starter were on the buffet, along with T-bone steaks and cake, which catered for those who could not tell the time of the day. A bleep indicated that a text message had arrived.

"Ingrid, CU at Grand Central NYC under the clock15.00 hours, L".

Ingrid had to move fast and leave most of the food which caused the maître d' to inquire whether something was amiss. She waved him away and told him to put it on her room costs before squeezing into a business suit. The only delays were the increasingly more complex searches to gain entry into the airside complex of cafes and expensive clothes nestling with Stetsons and dream catchers. Ingrid didn't carry her country and western outfits as she relied on Chuck and her manager to supply the equipment. It was under two hours flight to JFK but the limo took almost as long to Grand Central. New York taxi drivers were good at finding Grand Central which was probably why her meeting had been scheduled there.

Leonardo recognised Ingrid immediately. He had brought a flunky to carry the necessary luggage so that he was free to conduct business; they found a table in the vast station complex of food markets and cafes. Ingrid was issued with El Al tickets to Tel Aviv and an onward flight to Cairo where she would be met and given further instructions.

The times on the boarding passes gave little space for error as there was a three hour check-in process for El Al. She took the first train back to JFK and headed for the terminal. Her American passport seemed a good choice, with her security record doctored at the highest level to avoid delays. After a full body x ray and a comprehensive search of the little she had brought, the cross examination began.

She was going to Tel Aviv to teach some specialists. No, she had no terrorist connections and she was simply an academic with an international reputation and they could check her publications if they wanted. After an hour she was installed in business class alongside with some ultra-religious diamond dealers, with the long side locks and fringes issuing from beneath their shirts. Some passengers juggled their bulky bundles of possessions into the overhead containers; others stood in the aisles praying from battered black tomes and rhythmically swaying. Bags of rather smelly home-made food had been dumped precariously on seats. Their black fur hats, although perfect for the east European winters where they originated, were less suitable in the Middle-Eastern heat.

The bucket seats converted into slide down beds and, together with some Lynchburg special, Ingrid had a peaceful night, only to be woken with a choice from a menu prior to landing and another security check, despite having slept with an unknown number of sky marshals. She faced the same questions in a different order before she was couriered to the connecting flights queue. On landing in Tel Aviv she caught a flight to Cairo where the process was much simpler, as in this case Israel was getting rid of her and so was not too bothered what she was going to do, especially in an

Arab country. After a short flight, a swarthy man with an Arabic sign drove her to a five-star multi-storey hotel and a suite with a small elderly man in robes and a keffiyeh. The conversation took place in Arabic. She was supplied with a Saudi passport, credit cards and contact names. They drank Turkish coffee with sweet biscuits and he thanked her for obtaining medical supplies for Gaza before her driver took her to meet Rana who was to be her guide into Hamas-controlled territories. The concrete tunnels were rather anatomically challenging but Rana was slender and it was Ingrid whose compromised lungs were struggling. Once on the other side of the border and in Gaza, the hospital was only too happy to renew her acquaintance and show her all the surgery that they had performed. They didn't mention the ones that had gone wrong. After Ingrid had performed the surgery, Rana passed her on to a driver who supplied her with the appropriate robes for the road journey to Beersheba in the Negev desert, a town with the greatest number of chess masters in the world.

At the border they discussed chess and Ingrid explained that she was preparing for a forthcoming Olympiad and needed to hone her skills. After a shower she reverted to her business suit and headed for the bar and a man with an Israeli Defense League uniform. He was a colonel in the reserves and had a family in Haifa, where he worked as a structural engineer. Ingrid was posing as a model en route to a fashion show in Tel Aviv with a taste for Lynchburg whisky. Colonel Halevy was also fond of the same liquor and even fonder of Ingrid and her American background and southern drawl, which had been practised over the years. She couldn't understand why the Israelis wore uniforms socially, maybe it was to get admired, maybe for complimentary food and drink or maybe because they couldn't be bothered to wash their clothes. She lost no time in heading for Tel Aviv airport and caught a flight back to Copenhagen.

En route from Tel Aviv to Copenhagen, Ingrid was enjoying the idea of peace and relaxation back home. Her Porsche was in one piece and quiet Scandinavian roads were a welcome change. Back in Helsingborg, she spent an hour in the bath and then went down to the supermarket and the checkout with all the other supermodels. Her BlackBerry rang; it was Pontus.

'Long time no hear, Ingrid.'

'I've been on vacation, you know, all over the place. How are you?'

'I could tell you over dinner at this new fish restaurant in Malmo.'

'That sounds like a lovely idea.'

'I'll pick you up at seven then, OK.'

'Fine.'

Pontus was a senior policeman who had bailed Ingrid out of many a tight spot and who only knew little about her other lives. It was difficult for her to disguise her modelling as she was on every cover in Sweden and many others around the world, and so people rightly designated her as a VIP and she enjoyed hospitality just to be seen to be using the place. Pontus never took her for granted as he had seen what happened to those who had. His father was a senior politician in Stockholm and Pontus had often been a victim of those who felt passed over for promotion. What they didn't realise was that the reason his father was a public figure was his ability, and Pontus had inherited this. That was why Ingrid was the perfect foil for him, although he never overstepped the mark and would have hated to be seen as a threat or a potential suitor. Quite simply, no-one was in Ingrid's league.

The restaurant was in the grand style with reminders

about the duel origins of Malmo, as part Danish and currently Swedish. It was in the region known as Skane and its flag had both the yellow of Sweden and the red of Denmark as a reminder. The tables were polished wood, the plates were Royal Copenhagen, the cutlery was Georg Jensen, and the walls were covered with tapestries from Danish King Christian of blessed memory, also revered in Sweden. Their table was the best in the house, with views of the harbour and the bridge to Sweden. Although the fish was Scandinavian, the wine was French and the starters were complemented with seaweed mini-fish house specialities. It seemed that everyone knew the couple, just for different reasons but, if blackmail was on the menu, Pontus's father would be happy to clear things up, as he was minister for Europe.

'You look tired, Ingrid.'

'Oh, that's charming Pontus. You certainly know how to woo a lady. So do you. Is it all the foreign drug smugglers coming over from Poland?'

Pontus smiled; he was familiar with Ingrid's sharp wit, but she was watching the television in the corner.

'Am I boring you already?' asked Pontus.

She smiled as the news bar on CNN announced that the Israeli Defense League had gone into Gaza to find one of their army colonels who had been abducted during the night. Ingrid sighed and then smiled.

'Let's enjoy the fish,' she said as she smiled.

3

It was a short hop and Diogenes had spent most of the trip saying yes to malt whisky. It helped to ward off the tight band that gripped the base of his skull. Any further and the dose of whisky would have increased to a level where he appeared incoherent and he risked getting into arguments and drawing attention to himself. They were soon at Gatwick where he was in the line for passport control and a man in uniform came over, examined his British passport, and gestured towards a room with a table and chairs. The decor was cold, and cheap, official in style, and he was left on his own with his minimal hand luggage.

'Mr Jackson, can I ask you what the purpose of your trip was?' asked the official, fingering one of Diogenes's bogus passports.

'Just to see old acquaintances and catch up on the latest research data,' said Diogenes.

'Research data, in what particular line would that be?' asked the official looking impatient.

'Oh nanochemistry and nano-biotechnology, that is my field,' explained Diogenes.

'And you are here for what exact reason?' asked the official.

'The same sort of reasons, and I may catch a football match whilst I am here,' replied a rather bored Diogenes in need of another shot of whisky.

'Do you have anyone who can verify your line of work?' persisted the official.

'I do, but I am not able to,' said Diogenes looking impatient and agitated.

'Is there a reason for this?' asked the official becoming more suspicious.

'Oh yes, my work is classified, but you could ring

MI6 or CIA.'

The official was sweating and he adjusted his government shirt and detachable tie and left the room. Diogenes checked his watch and his BlackBerry and wondered how tenacious this rather ponderous official would turn out to be. Had the official been alerted by the stewardess on the plane, who had noticed his interest in the newspaper photograph? Was everyone a spy? How much would it take to bribe him, compared with the rest of Europe or elsewhere? There were many loyal UK citizens who were 100% certain that no UK official could be bribed, but his experience had taught him otherwise. Diogenes mused about doing an academic study on the cost ratios of bribing customs officials and building up league tables and trend analyses. He jotted down some figures and graphs and the rudiments of equations. The official returned and noticed his jottings.

'Can I have that please?' asked the official.

Diogenes passed over the piece of dog-eared paper and the official squinted over the figures.

'And this is?'

'Just some preliminary stuff about nano-spheric polymers,' lied Diogenes.

Diogenes was one of those rare birds who could justify his scientific thoughts to the highest level, and what might be seen as blue-skies thinking for some, was a brilliant breakthrough for him. Nobody liked people like this. The lay public, like the customs official, thought he was a smuggler, but when they couldn't figure out what he was smuggling or why they felt that they had been made to look like fools.

Diogenes had been liberated from the bureaucracy and was on the Gatwick express en route to the university, minus his dog-eared piece of paper, which he had deposited in one of the bins outside the airport.

The train was full of passengers with LGW on their cases; it was like a badge, and he wondered why some of them had such preposterous heaps of luggage whilst others just had a natty valise. It was "we've been all around the world" versus "we've just popped over to top-up our designer wardrobe and complete a deal". Some appeared not to have seen soap for months whilst others had not a hair out of place and smelt like a perfumery. Diogenes was an in-between man due to his frequent use of business lounges, and he headed into a pre-arranged central London hotel. As a member of the gold star scheme, he was always upgraded to a suite and on the way he had picked up some clothes from his tailor near Victoria station so as to freshen up. His employers were Western governments and they insisted that when he was in town he enjoyed nothing but the best of facilities as a reward for some of the hovels he had to endure in the field.

His contact at the university was one of his research students who was in line for a top grade PhD.

'Have you incorporated the Volopowski equation into the calculations, Marie?' asked Diogenes.

'I tried to, but it sent the dynamics into freefall and so I concocted one of my own,' said Marie.

'Excellent, I wondered if you would spot that. I think your project will take less time than we thought. Are you free tonight?' asked Diogenes who had somehow slipped into social mode. He felt relaxed with Marie; she had come to him as one of the most exciting young researchers in the field and he had agreed to take her under his wing after seeing her photograph; he was human after all.

Diogenes's BlackBerry made a buzzing noise, he had no time for ring tones, and it announced a text message which read, "something has come up, will meet you tomorrow outside the Munich clock at Old

Trafford at 2pm, L".

Diogenes was out of the door muttering about appointments but for Marie was this a eureka moment or was it a Juliet one? Diogenes appeared to have slipped back into automaton mode.

The green room at the Nelson's Column public house was crammed with business folk. In the corner, occupying his usual berth, was Mordechai McIntyre, literary agent to some of the more prominent authors. A single malt was ordered for Diogenes, along with a smoked salmon sandwich.

'You are a pain to track down; you know I sometimes believe that the stuff you send me is autobiographical. Maybe we should change genre,' said Mordechai.

Diogenes smiled as Mordechai pulled out a sheaf of manuscript covered with green marker pen. Diogenes had to be careful about which pseudonym he used but usually he tried to match them to the genre of his companion.

'That looks ominous,' said Diogenes.

'It's your plotting, it's going round in ever decreasing circles to nowhere again. You need to focus,' said the agent.

'That's how I think, Mordechai. What can I do?'

'Retire?' suggested Diogenes, with tongue in cheek.

'It's this nanochemistry palaver; I'm sure no reader will have a clue what you are on about,' said Mordechai.

'It doesn't really matter, I mean I don't expect readers to be nano-technology experts, it is just part of the story,' said Diogenes.

'It may be part of the story but couldn't we change it to something simpler like just plain chemistry?'

'Oh definitely not, but that will become apparent as the story moves on.'

Mordechai looked to be in a trance. He was not used to this type of author. All of the other authors on his list were very precious. He dressed like a latter day dandy with a velvet smoking jacket (even though he didn't smoke), with corduroy trousers and the latest in designer trainers. Diogenes knew that Mordechai's office was like a large manuscript cupboard that was never inspected by the fire brigade. Maybe that was why the Nelson's Column was where he most liked to spend his time; Diogenes's time was, however, rationed.

'Are we done now?' asked Diogenes.

Mordechai shrugged his shoulders. He did this a lot when he was lost for opinions, and with Diogenes he was always devoid of opinions. They occupied different worlds; it was arts versus science, but in the case of Diogenes his science was so off the wall that Mordechai felt that it was very close to fiction. Diogenes washed down his sandwich with single malt and smiled and fought his way through the rush hour to his hotel, where he threw himself on the bed and picked up *The New York Times*. He flicked through to the foreign news where he found a pertinent piece.

"Ahmed Al-Kabool, Syrian attaché to Russia, has been found dead in suspicious circumstances. An autopsy carried out failed to reveal any obvious cause of death. Samples were being sent for toxicology to Damascus. Witnesses have failed to reveal anything unusual in his vicinity and he is said to have been in robust health. Two Israeli diplomats have been asked to pack and leave Russia within 24 hours".

Diogenes was studying one of the notes in his envelope and found a ticket that had been left for him at Heathrow airport. He barely had enough time for two whiskies before the stewardess welcomed him to Manchester International Airport as the plane slithered to a slow pace, after probably one of the worst landings in peacetime and it was just after 2pm when he was able to switch on his BlackBerry, which told him that a man with a Crombie and a red baseball cap was waiting under the Munich clock at Old Trafford, the home of Manchester United Football Club. The problem with match days was that the crowds were so dense that they carried you in directions over which you had no control, and you could not ask directions. In addition, the police horses were trying to kettle you into other areas, and so it took some time before Diogenes and his colleague in the red baseball cap were safely in a box, being served food and whisky.

Manchester United were knocking the ball around with the aplomb that came with multi-million transfer fees whilst the other team were left chasing shadows.

'I thought this would be a suitable venue for you,' said Leonardo.

'Yes, it certainly makes a change,' said Diogenes.

A suitcase was produced and before the game had ended Diogenes was en route to Damascus via London Heathrow. He left early and luckily he had seen enough of play to be satisfied that Manchester United would have won and he was glad to be able to avoid the crowds. He thought it odd that the same person who was now using a Saudi passport could be travelling through the same airport as the one who had come in on a British one, but he still had the usual body searches afforded to swarthy men. In the circumstances, Diogenes was in another business suit when he arrived at Damascus airport and a waiting car took him to the Al-Raqi area of town, to be met by Tamuz Halevy and guided to a well-preserved block of rooms that must have dated back to when the Hebrews were prominent in Syrian society. Halevy explained that they were re-consecrating the synagogue in Damascus, with the full support of the government, and left Diogenes to fend for himself. Diogenes surveyed his bed, chair and table, wondering whether there was a rest room in the vicinity. There was a sweeping brush outside the door which helped in clearing the debris from the floor onto the landing. Diogenes opened his suitcase, extracted a laptop and plugged in a memory stick. The download was simply an electronic form of the envelope system but he also had his own memory stick which enabled him to transfer data to his BlackBerry. That was enough for the day. He transferred some whisky from the suitcase to his throat and fell asleep.

As promised on the laptop, there was a knock on the door at 8.30am and a tall, dark-haired slender girl with a loose veil announced that they were going to see the town. As they descended to the street he could see the extent of the damage as the pockmarked buildings from biblical times were interspersed with rubble and beggars with missing limbs, whilst underfoot there was sawdust where blood had been. Youths with Western T shirts and football strips were giving out leaflets. He had been warned not to get sucked in to any of the activity, as not only was it a scam, but also you never knew whether it was government sponsored. They settled in the Café Morocco where Diogenes ordered eggs and pitta bread with Turkish coffee; his guide just had the coffee. Diogenes had been told to adopt a Middle-Eastern persona and so they spoke in Arabic. It was difficult to know who was who in Syria and it was best to fear the worst. After the snack, Diogenes was taken by his companion through a maze of backstreets where there was less chaos to a meeting of the revolutionary council, so that they could exchange information and discuss ways forward. Food was eaten sitting on a rug and with fingers, although Diogenes noticed that several of those at the meeting did not have all their fingers, but they were friendly and supportive even though they did not know who he was. He listened intently as they outlined their need for Western help before a whole civilisation were wiped out by the dictator's forces.

There was a sound of gunfire outside; Diogenes recognised it and dived onto the floor, pulling his guide down with him, as he motioned for the others in the café to follow his example. He could see out of the corner of the window tracer shots ricocheting off stonework which made it difficult to get about during daylight. A dull thud followed by a sharp shriek told him the shooter had claimed a victim. But this was no routine attack. He saw that anyone who ventured out, perhaps from curiosity or ignorance, was hit within seconds. This was a sniper, government backed with a high velocity weapon and years of training. Diogenes searched for his BlackBerry; the bartender motioned for him to put it away for fear that it could be a target, but Diogenes just nodded and smiled with grim determination as he pressed buttons and whispered OK. He pressed the green button and after a few seconds the noise became random and wild, and then stopped. There was another thud as a uniformed body with a rifle landed on the road near where they had been eating. Diogenes moved to the door, to the disquiet of the terrified personnel, strode over to the twitching body and turned him onto his back. The sniper had camouflage fatigues with army insignia and short dark hair and where his eyes had been there were two dark holes. Diogenes smiled and returned to his food.

The council welcomed Diogenes with respect usually reserved for a great warrior. A map was produced, which outlined the state of play and the group pointed to the diagrams of weapons, tanks and an army.

'This is what we need, no-one can supply them, the international community cannot even declare its support for us and without this we are doomed. This is our chance for eternity and we are hoping for miracles from you,' said the leader.

Diogenes shook his head and stared at the Syrian flag and the photographs of martyrs around the walls. There were a few battle-worn Kalashnikovs and mortars but otherwise little of much use. He knew that the ammunition was often wasted by hot heads firing into the air, and the rest of the hardware was just for show. The committee looked brave but sad, as they knew that they were running out of time.

'I don't think I can supply any of this and even if I could it wouldn't last long; without planning and trained personnel, any intervention would set off World War Three. The Americans and NATO are already stretched,' said Diogenes.

Outside the room they could hear the rumbling of tanks and armoured jeeps combing the streets as the civilians ran for cover. Diogenes gently pulled back a curtain and pulled out his BlackBerry. The committee panicked and dived under the table as they waved to Diogenes not to turn on his device. Ignoring their concerns, he pointed it out of the window and pressed the keyboard. The tanks, jeeps and soldiers froze and there was an eerie silence. Diogenes left the room and took his companion's hand as they calmly walked back to his room. The night was long and full of action as the guide proved to be every bit as valuable as the Syrian national treasures, and Diogenes found that his every need was more than satisfied. He poured out some whisky and sighed.

'How did you do that?' asked his companion.

'What would that be?' asked Diogenes.

4

Ingrid was back at work in Malmo in Sweden. She carefully lowered the patient's eyeball onto his cheek. The theatre nurses had taken a minute electronic device from its vacuum-packed polythene sterile bag and deposited it into a kidney dish. This was not the district hospital in Malmo, but a special purpose-built module erected in the suburbs by the Bionic International Transplant Corporation, or BITS for short. The international staff were able to redeploy at short notice to wherever they were needed. Ingrid gently lifted the eyeball into position and, using a microscope, made a minute incision into the rear, near the optic nerve. She was familiar with these devices, having been trained by the Honourable Freddie McAloish of that Ilk, bionic engineer. The idea was that no organ was irreplaceable, and that it was just a matter of identifying the challenge, getting the robotics right, and then implanting it.

The part was carefully threaded into the eyeball using guide wires and then, with a revolutionary dispenser, the battery was implanted to an area behind the ear.

After her efforts, Ingrid sat in the lounge, catching up on which magazines were using her on the cover. Originally she had been spotted singing in a country music festival by one of the top Paris fashion houses when they were on the hunt for slender tall blue-eyed blondes. She had tried to shrug them off several times but they acquired her photograph from her music agent anyway, and the extra money was always useful to fund her research work.

Her BlackBerry rang.

'Hello, it's Freddie. Can you talk?'

'Always, to you, Freddie.'

They had linked up many times from when they first met at university when he had taken her under his wing. She had been mesmerised by his presence; he was by far the tallest and the most brilliant man she had ever seen and his knowledge was not just confined to bio-engineering, but seemed to be unlimited. She had never met someone like this before, either in Scandinavia or at Harvard, where she was polishing her microsurgical skills. Freddie seemed to be everywhere and his opinions were sought, not only from Harvard dons, but also internationally.

'How do you fancy Afghanistan?' asked Freddie.

'I can't say I've ever had it in my top ten holiday destinations. What are you going to do over there?' asked Ingrid.

'Well I've just perfected this amazing bit of hardware that I'm dying to get my hands onto and I've had this offer that I can't refuse,' said Freddie.

'Well if you can't then I can't. Brothers and sisters in arms, as they say in your country.'

'OK, meet me at terminal five in Heathrow by the information desk, at 16.00,' said Freddie.

Freddie didn't really have a country even though his blood line went back to the tenth century. There had been a battle in medieval times, and his ancestor picked the side that was destined to become a superpower and they had forever been ennobled. Freddie's life was inevitably linked to the talents that originated in childhood and possibly went back to one of his illustrious ancestors, and even as a child he converted his radio into a radar system. After Eton he was seconded to Harvard to study bio-engineering, and emerged as a don even before the other students had graduated.

Ingrid had noticed that he wore a blazer with the

30

family coat of arms and the motto, 'Omnia Possibilis Est', or 'Everything Is Possible'. Under the blazer could be anything from his pyjamas, through a T shirt, to the full blown black tie; it was his dress code. He was always carrying a small aluminium case which Ingrid felt identified him as not just a weirdo but an important contributor. Ingrid usually did what Freddie asked; she could trust him and there had been many occasions when her stunning looks had courted trouble and Freddie had been on hand to smooth things out with the minimum of fuss. Freddie was the only person with whom Ingrid would go to a place like Afghanistan.

From Heathrow they drove to Brize Norton, where a large military plane was waiting.

Freddie and Ingrid presented themselves to the military security.

'What is in that case sir?' asked the officer.

'It's to do with my work,' said Freddie.

'Can you put it in the hold? It would be much safer.'

'No I would prefer to keep it with me; it is very delicate and not replaceable.'

'I will have to ask you to open it then, sir,' invited the security man.

Freddie stood silently as he unlocked the case and opened it. There were lines of small boxes, some with electronic equipment, but others had body parts with wires and small batteries attached. The officer looked unsteady and turned pale green as she slumped to the floor. A colleague was focussing on a brain in a polythene bag with a tube attached when her eyes began to glaze, and Freddie gently pushed her to one side, so that she vomited over someone else, rather than his case. This scenario triggered an alert system, and Freddie was secured in handcuffs and bundled into a secure office. An official with a pad of paper and some forms arrived later. Ingrid had been allowed through with no hindrance.

'I am sorry sir, but I have to inform you that assaulting one of her majesty's officers can be punishable with anything up to life imprisonment. What do you have to say?' asked the official.

'Look I am sorry OK, but she was about to be sick on some vital research that has taken years to put together, and it could have changed things quite drastically. I think you will find that is the reason why I am going to Camp Bastion,' replied Freddie.

'I am afraid they all say that, but what I want to know is why you felt the need to obstruct an officer in his line of duty,' said the official. 'Just open the case for me, will you sir?'

'I have to warn you that the last time I did this two of your staff became ill,' pointed out Freddie.

'Don't threaten one of her majesty's officers. I am not asking, I am telling.'

Freddie shook his head, and gave the officer a telephone number and his full name with his titles of rank. Freddie was confined to a small interrogation suite but he could hear them quite clearly in the next room as their tone changed from being offhand to deferent with the words "yes sir" being repeated in more civil tones. A senior officer entered the room, and apologised before telling Freddie that he was free to get on the plane to Camp Bastion.

Camp Bastion was like a capsule in the middle of a pre-historic landscape. Their quarters were within the officers' accommodation, and they were welcomed with a hot British meal enough for about five large men. The next day the medical officer in charge provided them with a list of candidates for the specialised neurobionics supplied by BITS. After rehydrated bacon and egg, it was down to work on assessments, as each candidate's files were analysed for suitability.

A Taliban fighter was first; he had lost his hearing and needed implants. After the surgery, when he came round, he was able to communicate with Ingrid. He was one of the tribal leaders, and expressed his gratitude asking Ingrid if she would act as a go-between in some negotiations.

The paralysis cases were the most challenging, and Freddie had to be in the theatre to adjust the bionics live during the operations. Some of the cases could only be marginally improved but provided some ideas for Freddie to work on for the future. The army medics were out of their depth and many were suspicious of outsiders drafted in to assist. Ingrid and Freddie were used to this, and tended to accommodate it.

Lunch was in the officers' mess with senior RAMC personnel, who were often even more suspicious than the other ranks. Freddie had experience of this in his rise to the top of his profession in the UK, although in the USA they did not seem have this problem. This was new for Ingrid and irritated her, particularly when it spread to sexism. She was worried that the next step was to undermine her, but she knew that Freddie would deal with that. Often, when they were operating, staff would pretend not to hear a request to hand her an implement, when there was a need for quick action. Others would drop expensive instruments on the floor. This was inevitably followed by an exaggerated apology and a wry smile to friends. Ingrid wondered why such twisted people had gone into a caring profession but Freddie pointed out that it was par for the course. He speculated that there would be hardly anyone left to do the work if caring was the sole qualification, as money and status were usually high on the list.

Freddie did not need to work, as the income from his estates in the new and old world brought in more than enough to be a playboy. Ingrid was a playgirl but she had to work to sustain her lifestyle.

Ingrid received a text on her BlackBerry and headed to the UK. The Foreign Office always issued terse statements and a six-word sentence named the contact, the date and the time. Luckily, Ingrid did not cause as much security concern as Freddie, and after a night in a government-arranged London hotel she was in the waiting area in the Foreign Office for an audience with Leonardo. She was ushered in to a room which had a ceiling dating back to when prominent Englishmen thought themselves near to heaven. It was wood panelled with enormous windows with office furniture designed for large meetings. Leonardo opened a case to reveal a sheet of paper marked top secret and put it on the desk in front of him as he perused it, apparently for the first time. He looked up to her and asked her, rather incongruously, whether she knew what this was about.

The note read: "The Foreign Secretary has asked that you use your contacts to avail us of any possible fruitful dialogues with the Arab states that may further the interests of the UK and vis-à-vis the EU, NATO and the UN. It goes without saying that this must be kept at the highest level of secrecy".

Leonardo stared at the note through his half-moon glasses, and then at her.

'Is that clear, madam?'

'Oh crystal clear, sir. But just one query, if I may, sir?'

'Anything, anything at all,' he said, as he smiled in a rather obsequious manner.

'It is a tad vague, as it stands, sir. I was wondering if the Foreign Secretary had any specifics in mind?' asked Ingrid.

Ingrid was used to the world of medicine, country music and fashion but international espionage was an area in which she had never expressed any interest.

'Oh no madam, I can assure you HMG never has any specifics in mind,' explained Leonardo.

Ingrid rose to leave and heard some clearing of the throat. Leonardo handed her the envelope and nodded, as he pressed a buzzer to summon a gentleman with medal ribbons and a uniform, who accompanied her back to the street.

She was supplied with the appropriate papers and business class tickets on the next flight to Cairo, where she was met by a swarthy but clean-shaven man in a suit. The journey from the airport in the Mercedes was smooth and quiet, apart from the background Arabic music. The darkened windows made sure that she was not disturbed whilst the traffic police waved them through the camels, donkeys, three-wheel taxis and armoured cars. His Excellency, the British under-secretary for Education, met them at a large wooden door scarred with assorted bullet holes, dents and slashes.

In a room that had once been rather grand, she was invited to sit in an old wooden chair as the under-secretary, with white whiskers and a cream crumpled suit, struggled with the flies in the oppressive humidity. He gestured to a small fat man with a fez, who brought in some juice and sweet Arab delicacies. The room was not air conditioned, possibly due to a large metal box dangling from a single rusty wire outside the window. Closer inspection would have revealed part of a shell case protruding from the box. The under-secretary observed Ingrid glancing at the anomaly and he also observed that, unlike most of them, she was not sweating.

'Firstly can I re-assure you that the shell is not live?

Cecil who brought you up was with the desert rats during the war and knows about these matters. May I also apologise, madam, for bringing you to such an inhospitable place. I would not have asked if we were not desperate. You will know what a mess this part of the world has become. They would like to blame the British, but this time I don't think even we can claim to be responsible. I do know of your background, but more importantly of the esteem in which you are held in these parts and no doubt in many others.'

'That is very flattering, your Excellency,' said Ingrid.

The diplomat was, by appearance, also ex-forces, and had had many postings, and even more crates of gin and tonic in his time. The one survivor from all the turmoil in the embassy was the portrait of the Queen, but also there were several silver cups and statuettes of men holding pistols. Ingrid could see why the old fellow had stayed at his post for so long.

'I have a mission for you, and I wouldn't ask, but I can't think of anyone else who is capable of seeing this through,' said the under-secretary.

'Well I certainly am your woman, as they say in your country,' said Ingrid.

'I am going to arrange for you to be appointed as Minister of Health here in Cairo. I have your papers and you will have an office and staff, but more importantly, you will have a licence to roam.'

'But what of the various factions within Egypt, will they accept me as bona fide?'

'I have taken care of all this and you have diplomatic status and even the use of a private plane, but I would caution you about over-using this, as it raises suspicion.'

'Is there anything specific I need to do?'

'I would not overly concern yourself about that, as

the place is so corrupt that they are used to those even at the highest level, either doing nothing, or stealing and murdering. Just follow your nose.'

'And so, what do you recommend?' asked Ingrid.

'Just one piece of advice, chin up,' said the under-secretary.

5

Tamuz Halevy had returned to his house and the centuries of decay when it struck him that he hadn't heard from Diogenes. He had felt a bit guilty when the British authorities had asked him to act as a go-between, due to his local knowledge, but although nobody in Syria could have been more local than himself, he realised that the reputation of the rest of the Syrians was not what it had been in biblical times. He wondered whether it was wise to go back to where he had deposited Diogenes in a safe house, but he had second thoughts as he knew little about him and may have made things worse.

Most of Diogenes's friends told him that his main problem was his neurosis and that was why he had very few people that he bothered to call a friend. He had been raised in an obscure English village, to a family who had far too many brain cells to go round. Some of them went on to an education, but others were either put into care or chose other routes. Diogenes had joined the army to avoid further schooling, but after several of his commandants found him impossible to discipline they sponsored him to study nanopolymers in London. Even his supervisors were in awe at the quality and quantity of his work and before long he was becoming widely published and cited by world acclaimed scientists. After this, news reached the army high command, who, after some high level discourse with his academic supervisors, came to the conclusion that it was best for him to be fast-tracked to the intelligence corps, and he became a freelance scientist collaborating on weaponry and blue skies research.

Tamuz Halevy had still not made any decision about what to do about his missing scientist and he was drawing diagrams on the back of a packet of the finest Turkish cheroots when Diogenes burst through his front door, fiddling with his BlackBerry.

'I need food and drink urgently, I don't know how you have survived in this place; can you help?' said Diogenes in a stressed state as he held his neck in his hand to fight off the pain.

'I need you to go -------' said Tamuz Halevy.

'No, food and whisky and cigarettes: that's what I need, everything else has to go on the back-burner,' said Diogenes.

Halevy shrugged; he often did this when he was lost for words. Syrian Jews were few and far between as most of them had fled to neighbouring countries and then on to Spain or Portugal, where the inquisition drove them to Northern Europe. Halevy was either too stupid or he was extremely wise to stay put and wheel and deal himself around the backstreets of Damascus. Halevy was dressed as a street Arab, and it was probably his outward nondescript appearance that ensured his own longevity from a family line that had lasted several centuries.

The Café Morocco in Damascus had bits of masonry coming through the ceiling and some mortar holes stuffed with newspaper. Eggs were served with pitta bread and coffee and were an appetising alternative to sheep's brains in aspic. Halevy just stared vacantly as the manager winked at Diogenes and his gargantuan appetite. Most of his other customers did not eat but quietly sat drinking and smoking as they chatted. It was quiet in the café, as the government forces ate at other places, and Halevy began to sketch his grand plan on a serviette in between mouthfuls.

'I have a message from one of my contacts in the holy land; it would seem that they have some difficulty with one of their compatriots,' said Halevy.

Halevy spoke in out-of-date English from his time fighting with and against the British forces in Palestine, but its origins were from the crusader era. All the years Diogenes had spent with his science had only served to make him more intolerant of small talk. For him to be closeted in a grubby café with some street Arabs in a haze of food and smoke was building up his inner tension and making him feel like running out into the street and risking a sniper's bullet.

'It would seem that one of the Israeli Defense Force officers has been spirited out of a base in Beersheba, and is in the hands of the enemy forces. The usual contacts have failed to make any contact and there is no ransom demand or threat involved. They have asked me to find someone to volunteer to cross enemy lines,' said Tamuz Halevy.

'What makes you feel that I am your man?' asked Diogenes.

Halevy looked at Diogenes with a benign desperate expression which comes from centuries on the run, evading everyone and trusting no-one.

'I have papers for you that will get you into Gaza as a Syrian citizen trading in precious metals and the rest is up to you. Your contact will meet you on the other side; he is an ally and an altogether decent chap,' said Tamuz.

They left the Café Morocco by the back door and Diogenes was saddened to see heaps of animal carcasses and empty boxes with rusting cans in between a thriving rat colony. They found Tamuz Halevy's Land Rover and, after kicking some debris away, they set off on their mission.

Diogenes was not sure how many kilometres of desert and shanty towns he passed through, but it was different from business class. At certain stops they would pick up some traditional Arab food as they evaded forces who might ask too many questions. At any check point Diogenes was just another Arab labourer coming back home from the work that the Israelis wouldn't do. After an hour they found an old Crusader fort with some market stalls and their contact was waiting for customers interested in military hardware. He greeted Tamuz Halevy in the traditional way, waved over a youth carrying a Kalashnikov to mind his stall.

'I have set up some meetings for you. I understand that you have been asked to track an IDF colonel who was spirited over to us a short time ago. I do not know the man personally but I know of him; he is in a fishing village in the south, but you will need to be clever to get near to him. From what I hear that is very much up your street,' said the contact.

'How do I travel?' asked Diogenes.

'There is a moped outside, you have money and papers and I leave the rest to you. My contact down there is just known as Mamser Ha-erev or Mamser for short.'

Diogenes knew enough Yiddish to realise that Mamser meant bastard, and Mamser Ha-erev was bastard of the night.

Diogenes was quite adept at moped riding in the Middle East and before long he had reached the coast and felt dusty, stiff and in need of his staple whisky. There were numerous bars on the coast and whisky was in good supply. Cigars were cheap and before long he became a fixture in the area, with his new persona. This was part of his life now and he would change apartments as quickly as he changed acquaintances. Occasionally he would be followed and although he couldn't see anyone he knew they were there. On one occasion he had stopped to find an icon on his BlackBerry as he heard the footsteps get nearer, he pressed the green button and there was a dull thud about two metres away in the dark. He moved close enough to observe the man twitching and observe black holes in his eye sockets and continued to his bed whilst making a mental note to move on in the morning. As he adjusted his BlackBerry to the normal position he noticed an email.

'Meet you in the old souk at two pm, Mamser.'

A dark man in a crumpled suit was waiting for Diogenes.

'We meet at last, I am known as Mamser Ha-erev, I recognise you from your description. We have quite a complicated journey, not so far but very risky. But I know you are used to this.'

'Where are we going?' asked Diogenes.

'As with everything, I cannot say, partly because I don't wish to, but also because I only know part of it,' announced Mamser.

Mamser's ageing Fiat had been constructed from cannibalised parts, but the dented and filled bodywork did not matter in a country that had few rules and no rust. The roads were largely rubble with some areas of tarmac that the Israelis had despoiled on one of their sorties in retaliation for some mortar attacks. The seats were skeletal but Mamser could steer through the worst of the tracks by touch. Diogenes was not in the mood to make small talk and Mamser was in no mood to listen. Diogenes fished out his BlackBerry and was furiously tapping out numbers and Greek lettering. From time to time he would either nod or whine. Their arrival at the final destination coincided with Diogenes's end point in his work. They parked beneath some olive trees round the back of an old stone hut. Mamser quietly left the car and observed a group of men deep in conversation; they spoke Arabic and were arguing and banging the table. Mamser signalled to Diogenes to follow him.

'There is your quarry, the one in the T shirt with a Kalashnikov on the front and the logo "Red Army World Tour" on the back with a list of the battles on the reverse,' whispered Mamser. 'They are discussing a raid on a bus full of Israeli schoolchildren, the men are reluctant as it may lose them credibility with the more moderate Arab states, but the man in the T shirt is keen,' continued Mamser.

'What are you, chickens? I have been over there, I know how they think. Threats and a few mortars they can deal with, but mass action is the only way to make them change,' said the tall man in a T shirt.

Mamser produced some gasmasks and crept into the room letting off tear gas grenades. As they all dived for the floor, he shot them all in the back of the neck with his British army pistol, except for the T shirt man, whom he handcuffed and led out to the car and drove to a safe house, where all three disembarked. The T shirt man was the first to speak.

'Who are you and why have you brought me here?'

'We know your identity colonel,' said Mamser.

'I have no business with you, Jewish scum,' said the colonel.

'I am afraid that is about to change,' said Mamser.

'You can believe what you like but I am determined to see all of you dead,' said the colonel.

'I would love to oblige you but this is not part of my instructions, so you have no choice. You see I have even been thoughtful enough to provide you with a taxi service,' said Mamser.

'You will never get me anywhere in that, you can cuff me, gag me or knock me out but they will never let you over the border,' said the colonel.

Diogenes was smiling at the colonel's attempt at amateur dramatics; Diogenes was a professional, not a toy soldier strutting about firing his Kalashnikov in the air and wearing his prowess on a cheap T shirt. He was fiddling with his BlackBerry, whilst Mamser was thinking out the logistics.

'Don't worry I'll sort it,' said Diogenes.

He tapped out some codes and pressed the green button and watched the colonel's face morph into a fatuous expression. Mamser gazed at what had happened with his mouth open and Diogenes spoke to the colonel for the first time.

'You were saying?' said Diogenes.

'I can't quite recall,' said the colonel.

'About not wanting to go with us?' said Diogenes.

'I would be delighted to go with you, I just don't know why, but you seem to be the embodiment of god,' said the colonel.

'Is there anything we can get you?' asked Mamser.

'Yes, loaves and fish, I wish for a dish. I like your car, will it go far, have you a cigar?' said the colonel.

'What on earth have you done to him; how long will it last?' asked Mamser.

'Well I'm working on that, so I can't tell you at the moment,' said Diogenes.

Diogenes carried on scrolling and pressing buttons on his BlackBerry as the colonel muttered incomprehensively to himself with a fixed grin. Mamser drove on shaking his head and muttering.

'You must tell me something about what is happening,' said Mamser

'How about abnormal salience,' said Diogenes.

'Salience?' asked Mamser.

'Aliens,' shouted the colonel.

'No, salience. It is the manner in which an object can be similar but different from another and we are able to detect this now on a BlackBerry and log-on to alter it,' said Diogenes.

He knew that it went over most people's heads and

tried his best to avoid using jargon if he could, but he calculated that if he just ignored the questions, it took longer to get others to help him.

It worked and there was silence for the rest of the trip.

6

Ingrid, the new Egyptian Minister of Health, was re-arranging the furniture in her office. It consisted of artefacts from one of the Pharaohs in a neo-colonial setting and the room was the size of most people's homes, with columns and a ceiling decorated with Italianate friezes. She picked up a lump of alabaster from the mantelpiece expecting to see 'Made in Korea' underneath; she didn't. A servant knocked and entered, bowing repeatedly, and she nodded in his direction.

'Please your excellency, the prime minister wishes for your attendance at the weekly cabinet meeting,' said the robed figure with an ornate fez adorned with a polished gold badge.

Ingrid nodded again and prodded at the computer as the servant waited for some reaction from his new mistress. Should she reply, speak, move or even smile, it was a new experience for her to be in the position of an oriental potentate. He helped by moving his upturned hands and nodding towards the door, as if to say come this way. This process was interrupted by the sound of a text message from Chuck, her country music colleague, saying that she should contact him ASAP. Ingrid was in two minds; which was more important? She made an executive decision and texted Chuck to say she will come back to him in thirty minutes.

The cabinet room had once been quite magnificent with ornate stucco walls in bright oriental colours and masses of gilding. Due to years of use, it stunk of old tobacco and spirits, and the chairs were faded into the universal colour of worn-out. A variety of cabinet members of a different hue were arranged around the battered ancient table, from Nubians to albinos and from Moslems, via Coptic Christians, to even some

Jews and to Ingrid, a Scandinavian. The prime minister entered with his under-secretaries and assistants. Everyone was aware that the next day they could all be in jail, exile or shot, but in a fractured country like modern day Egypt, this was the norm. The agenda was read out, the minutes were accepted and the agenda items commenced. The prime minister began:

'Firstly I would like to introduce the new Minister of Health, Ingrid. She is an eminent doctor who will enhance our efforts to gain some global credibility in a world where it is in short supply, especially in the Arab world. Can you say a few words please Ingrid?' said the prime minister.

'Yes, thank you for inviting me to your ancient country; it is a pleasure for me to be here. I am here to support the prime minister in his ambitions for Egypt and the Arab world. I think he has captured the essential aspects of moving an ancient civilisation into the modern society and it has become obvious that nationalism must now be second to our aspirations, whether in health, or in the wider sense, as we look towards Europe and the USA as role models for a progressive picture,' said Ingrid.

The temperature was into the forties as the aging fans, riveted to the ceiling, had been taken over by flies. The noise of their efforts drowned out a lot of the conversation, which, along with the high tone deafness that comes with age, had meant that much legislation was passed on the nod with little understanding behind the decisions. Amidst the noise there was a call for cold drinks and a portly retainer struggled in with a bottle, glasses and some ice cubes of dubious provenance. The Minister of Defence seemed to dry up faster than most as he gripped the bottle and began to pour as he wished the prime minister would relocate to one of the cooler regions for the next few months.

Before any more items could be discussed, Ingrid noticed that there was a brief eerie silence, and then a rumbling before a massive blast blew out all the windows. The cabinet members remained seated, waiting for orders to do otherwise, whilst Ingrid dived under the table. When she emerged, amongst the dust and rubble, the members were simply brushing themselves down and moving debris off the table.

It took some hours for the building to be evacuated and the cabinet relocated to the local emergency ward where Ingrid, now in her theatre greens, was supervising the medical response. The prime minister had survived, but with loss of movement in his lower limbs.

'I need to enlist the help of my friend Freddie in this, if I have your permission,' said Ingrid to the maimed but conscious prime minister.

'Whatever you need is yours, money is no barrier, we will find the one who did this and execute him,' said the prime minister.

'If I may be so bold, the modern response, sir, is we will bring them to justice, which may mean the same but it sounds a little softer, yes?' said Ingrid. 'But meanwhile your health is the priority.'

'Oh yes, of course Ingrid, you see I am learning already.'

Freddie had arrived at Cairo airport, having flung some things in a bag, but was having difficulty with his hand luggage. The customs officials had selected him for a prolonged interrogation on the basis that he stuck out from the rest of the travellers with his extreme height and fair skin. They were pouring over the contents of his scientific case and chattering as they brought in officials with increasing amounts of gold braid on their epaulettes. Freddie's explanations didn't make any sense to them and despite all his efforts they were determined to link him to weapons or illicit drugs. The dogs started to behave in a rather embarrassing manner not seen before and this left the officials with no alternative but to detain Freddie. He texted Ingrid and explained his dilemma.

'I apologise for troubling you, prime minister, but you remember my friend Freddie who is going to help me with your surgery, well he is being held up at the airport by some officials over his hand luggage. They think he is trying to smuggle in a bomb,' said Ingrid.

'What, a bomb? Who are we employing there? I thought I had covered all of this with the immigration minister. Can you get him on the line for me please?' said the prime minister.

'I think he was blown up in our cabinet meeting and he is in another ward,' said Ingrid.

'OK Ingrid, you can assume the portfolio temporarily; can you get me some headed paper and just fire the official and get your colleague here ASAP,' said the prime minister as he signed the paper.

The operating theatre was buzzing, not only with staff, but also with onlookers, keen to see the new minister in action. She worked silently with Freddie, who improvised on the spot, as she cut and prepared the prime ministerial spine for some ground breaking work. Freddie had his own table, with his sterile kit being used to cut the material and bionics to fit the area of damage. In the room adjacent to the theatre suite, Ingrid used the natural break in proceedings, and in her other persona as Sue Dakota, country music legend, she was texting Chuck about his earlier call. It was the middle of the night in Tennessee, but Chuck never slept and when he heard the message coming through he was on alert with his texting finger.

"What kept you, Sue?"

"Oh just a little local trouble that I needed to sort,

Chuck."

"I got a real biggie here for you if you can get over."

"Sounds exciting, shoot."

"Well no-one other than the President is holding this grand gig for some kids' charity internationally and it's going to be country music, and guess what?"

"What?" asked Sue.

"Just that he has gotten your all-time favourite, T-Bone Redneck and his Galveston Rebels to participate and we have been asked to pen a special number for the occasion, with royalties going to the charity."

"You've done it again, Chuck. I am up for that, when is it?" asked Sue.

"Tomorrow night."

"Look, I am a bit stuck here but I promise that I will get back to you when I am done," texted Sue.

Ingrid wrapped up the operation along with Freddie and his stem cell mixtures and she was back in her ministerial residence when she heard that the prime minister was making a speedy recovery and Freddie had been appointed Minister of Defence. She was busy writing some lyrics to take with her to Washington DC and she knew that Chuck would deal with the music side; it was a partnership made in country music heaven.

'I'm just your country love/making time to be like one/why can't we be with each other/just country love,' she wrote.

'We started in Jackson goin' on Baton Rouge/just bein' love together/on the good ole Missisip'/up to New Orleans/

'We just ate Cajun crawfish/and gumbo pie/ but we was eatin' each other/as our love flew by/

'I'm just your country love/making time to be like one/why can't we be with each other/just country love/'

There was plenty more where that came from but

she could make any changes on the flight over. She smiled at the prospect of catching up with T-Bone Redneck. He was three hundred and fifty pounds and six foot nine, without his cowboy boots, which had to be hand-lasted for durability and size. Legend had it that only everglade 'gater horny-backs could provide the stiffening required for his boots and particularly pregnant female ones. T-Bone enjoyed fishing out his own 'gaters on his ranch in Oklahoma, and with one heel on its neck he would throttle it with a throwing rope.

Ingrid had morphed into Sue Dakota on the plane and before long and after a brief check-in at a local motel she had caught up with T-Bone in a bar behind the Washington venue and the Tennessee whisky was flowing liberally.

'Hi y'all T-Bone what's movin' down there in Okey?' said Sue.

'We been playin' a lot at all the meets and shiftin' the ole red-eye like it's goin' out of fashion,' said T-Bone.

'But what brings you to Yankee country?' asked Sue.

'Well jess like y'all, we had the call.'

Sue didn't mention her recent ministerial elevation, so she concentrated on looking pretty with her natural cowgirl looks for a change, and strummed her guitar. The red carpet and the celebs had all turned out and written their cheques as Mr President and his entourage were ushered in to the main box and introduced to some of the selected few, mainly the organisers. Everyone talked about the all-American heritage of country music being the closest they had to a history of their own. The master of ceremonies was a golden oldie, brought up in a shack near a dirt track in Alabama, who had his first guitar made from an old washboard and the remains of a cat. Some film footage of the good old days, with white whiskers and cows and hens, started off the show and this was accompanied by some hits from the thirties. After this there was live music from modern day heart-throbs with the Stetsons suitably sanitised for the President and the charitable guests. After whupping the crowd into excitement, some oldies staggered on to the platform to applause from all. The grand finale was Sue and Chuck and a new number, but all eyes were on Sue, who made the number a little superfluous and she milked it with an inflexion and a smile while she waved to friends in the hall. Then T-Bone and his band strutted on first with their guitars, washboards, fiddle players and concertina. The band came out wearing Confederate troopers uniforms with a kepi, but as the music struck up, on strode T-Bone in the light greys with an officer's Stetson with tassels shouting 'One day the South will rise again'.

On seeing this in Washington, the Yankees maintained an embarrassed silence. This was followed by rebel songs, complete with T-Bone's anecdote about his great grandpappy having been slaughtered by the blue bellies at Franklin, Tennessee, along with about half a dozen Confederate generals, heroes to a man. With T-Bone's bulk and his rockabilly style, he could only stand out, and some even seemed to secretly be tapping along with the rhythm. One thing was for sure, was that for just a brief period, the south had risen again, the beautiful south at that.

T-Bone and the Galveston Rebels skipped the farewell party and repaired to the bar over the road with their own supply of Tennessee special with some of the more independent-minded southern musicians. Sue was interested in T-Bone's hat; she liked hats.

'Where you get that fine specimen, T-Bone?'

'Which one would that be?'

'The one on yer head,' said Sue.

'As I said, this was my great grandpappy's. Look at this here bullet hole complete with blood and all. Took him to his grave like a true patriot,' said T-Bone.

'There ain't no blood in that, it must have been a bloodless coup back there in Franklin?' said Sue.

'I swear on the beating hearts of my kinfolk, this was his hat, and I am his kin.'

'Anyways T-Bone, what you tryin' to do out there?' asked Sue.

'We need to show them Yankee bastards whose land this is. We got all the oil, all the mining, all the fish, all the cows and most of all, all the men.'

'Yeah?'

'Yeah and we need to get rid of the lily-livered liberals running this place on Capitol Hill and all their appeasin' ways.'

'You planning on a revolution, T-Bone?'

'If I have to. They stole our country and they bin lootin' and rapin' ever since.'

Sue's phone made a noise and a text appeared.

"There is a revolution kicking off here, we need you, Freddie, MOD, Cairo".

7

Diogenes was the front seat passenger in the ageing Fiat with Mamser driving and the colonel in the back seat smiling to himself and muttering incomprehensible rhymes. Occasionally Mamser would throw a cookie towards the colonel from the glove compartment which he wolfed down with copious streams of saliva and grunting noises. Mamser just shook his head and glanced at Diogenes who was busy re-programming his BlackBerry. They were driving down roads which Diogenes imagined were similar to the surface of the moon and he wondered how Mamser found his way through the terrain. Mamser just shrugged when asked to explain his orienteering skills, but Diogenes wondered whether this was so that the colonel could not gain any advantage, but possibly in his role as international courier, Mamser was used to listening and not talking.

Diogenes noticed that the rubble and discarded rusting weapon parts were giving way to a form of road and the sight of uniformed men made his head feel tight. He rummaged through what belongings he had brought for any sign of whisky or cigarettes, without any success, before the colonel offered him a cigarette and a light whilst muttering "cig, pig, trigger." Mamser took a small plastic tub and rubbed some of the cream on the back of his neck as they approached the border. At the border the guards took a quick glance and, on noticing the back seat passenger, just nodded, and waved them through without asking for papers which Halevy had prepared earlier.

'What was in the tub?' asked Diogenes.

'Let's call it essence of camel shit,' said Mamser.

Tamuz Halevy met them at the Café Morocco on the

Israeli side for a hand-over whilst they left the colonel in the car with a cookie packet. Halevy peaked in to the car to check on the colonel, who was thrusting the cookies into his mouth by the handful, before Mamser grabbed most of them off him for safety reasons. Tamuz Halevy stood in the baking heat with his mouth open, in a state of shock.

'What did they do to him, poor sod?' asked Tamuz.

'I think you'll find it's a little more complex than you expected,' said Mamser.

'But he is a decorated serving soldier in the IDF, highly respected by his men and known for his bravery,' said Tamuz.

'I think you actually mean was, past tense,' said Mamser.

'He must have gone through a lot. I am sure the President will want to honour him for his efforts when we get him back,' Said Tamuz.

Diogenes smiled as he visualised the awards ceremony.

Mamser did not argue but finished his coffee and winked at Diogenes. The BlackBerry buzzed and a message came through for Diogenes's next mission. Diogenes was scrolling through his orders as the colonel was moved to Halevy's car, with a bottle of water and little more than a wide grin as he had begun to strip his clothes off. Halevy just nodded and drove off with a sheet over his passenger.

The BlackBerry informed Diogenes that he was wanted in Geneva for the next mission and the timescale gave him enough time check into a hotel in Tel Aviv, dive into a bath to remove Mamser's camel odour and stock up with cigarettes and single malt. He tuned into CNN and noticed the rolling news bar had announced that a brave Israeli patriot had been spirited out of enemy hands in a daring mission, without loss of

Israeli life, and was now back in Israel being debriefed and enjoying visits from his family. The next morning Diogenes was queuing to board a flight to Geneva. On disembarkation he was fast-tracked to a short queue to meet a border official.

'What is the purpose of your visit to Switzerland?' asked the border official.

'I have a meeting with some of your European representatives,' said Diogenes.

'About what, in particular?' asked the official.

'My main line of business,' said Diogenes.

'And that would be?' asked the official.

'That would be confidential,' said Diogenes.

'That is not satisfactory, I am afraid my colleague will need to have more detail. Just wait in this room,' said the official.

'Look this happens every time I come here. Don't you check your records? I'll save you some time; I deal in nanochemistry and nanobiodynamics. The chairman of the European science committee will be happy to give you more details, here is his card,' said Diogenes losing patience.

'Are you trying to make fools of us? Just see how we deal with this,' said the irate official.

Diogenes was bundled into a side room and strip-searched before being told to sit on a rather uncomfortable bench, usually reserved for terrorists.

'I am entitled to a phone call,' said Diogenes.

He was supplied with a cracked old phone which seemed to get through to the same French message no matter what number was dialled. A muscular giant of a man with multiple medal ribbons entered the room and grabbed him by the collar and escorted him and the phone back to the room. After twenty minutes there was a noise outside of French officials and guards. The volume increased as the door burst open and Diogenes was escorted into a waiting corps diplomatique Mercedes.

'Can something be done about these people in the airport?' asked Diogenes.

'Here take this,' said the driver as he passed him a bottle of whisky and some cigarettes.

The driver also gave him an envelope which contained a CD card, some documentation and yet another passport, to smooth his way around the globe. He arrived half an hour late for his appointment at the Clinique Plastique de Genève with an apology and a headache, but no real explanation for his delay.

He was met in the clinic by a blonde nurse who seemed to be willing to speak any language he chose. The procedure was painlessly performed by a suave genito-urinary specialist and after an hour he was on his way with a box of antibiotics and some painkillers, to a multi-story glass structure, after his driver briefly dropped him off to check in to a hotel. He was escorted via a rather complex escalator system to a spotless, minimalist office where a high-ranking European official offered him a vast leather armchair.

'I have arranged for you to meet some of our boffins again for some equation talk, here are the times and venues,' said the official.

'Thank you, it looks as if there is a biggie coming up, can you tell me anything?' asked Diogenes.

'I was hoping that you would be able to answer that one after you have met our hand-picked scientists,' said the official.

The university nano laboratory was in need of some repair as it had been created from the then redundant politics annexe when the old Soviet studies department was closed when the Berlin wall came down. Ironically it had been named (unofficially) the Gorbachov unit, but these days, rather than old KGB material, it was full of screens of never-ending data and white-coated post-graduates analysing the material. The head of department, Professor Bi, greeted Diogenes.

'You have any specifics in mind?' asked the professor.

'Yes, I am looking at linking brain receptors and nano-receptors,' said Diogenes.

'But this has not even been thought of,' said the professor.

'But I am thinking of it now and it is quite urgent,' said Diogenes.

'How urgent?' asked the professor.

'A week or so at most,' said Diogenes.

The professor rubbed his forehead and his eyes began to flicker as if he was about to have a seizure. He was small in stature and worryingly pale and thin and Diogenes wondered whether the man was so dedicated to his work that he sometimes forgot to eat. He had seen this before in his academic journeys and indeed there were times when he forgot about the mundane matters of life. Diogenes found a tube of sugar-rich fruit drops in his pocket and he offered one to the professor who put it in his mouth without even looking at it.

'We couldn't even dream of achieving that in even months and maybe years,' said the professor sucking on his fruit drop.

Diogenes took out his BlackBerry and moved the cursor up and down some lists whilst typing in some new data.

'You see, professor, we are using glutamate receptors which we think is the route in to enabling us to manipulate brain systems by external electronics,' said Diogenes.

'You mean you have tapped into the impulses?' asked the professor who was looking less cadaverous.

'Not only tapped in, that was two years ago, but now we can use them and if you look at one of these apps, you can see the electronic wave form, which shows that there is a link,' said Diogenes.

'So how can we help you?' asked the professor.

'I need you to refine this linkage, which I will download for you, and let me have the chance to modify it, based on clinical responses, certainly on primates and also with some volunteers. It looks like you have plenty of volunteers in here alone, who would crave for their names in a prestigious journal, although we will have to delay that for political reasons,' said Diogenes.

The professor was not used to being told what to do. His life experience had begun in a corrugated iron shack by a rice plantation that had been worked by his family for generations. He attended regional school number 382828 but had been marked out as somebody special after gaining full marks for everything that had been put in front of him.

Diogenes's telephone rang:

'Hello this is Halevy, do you mind talking to this IDF doctor about our recent travelling companion?'

'Not at all,' said Diogenes.

'Hello, I am General Cohen head of army mental health. We are a little puzzled about the mental state of the gentleman whom you kindly delivered to us.'

'How can I help you?' asked Diogenes.

'Well, have you given him any medication?' asked the general.

'No I am not a medical doctor,' said Diogenes.

'Didn't you notice something strange about him?' asked the general.

'He seemed a bit quiet, but I thought it might be due to all the trauma of his abduction and captivity. Has he said anything about it?' asked Diogenes.

'No, on the contrary he is anything but quiet, he is just rambling nonsense and behaving like an animal,' said the general who was becoming rather impatient.

'Is this out of the ordinary for him?' asked Diogenes.

'Out of the ordinary, he was a highly trained intelligence officer with many awards for bravery and devotion to duty,' said the general.

'OK, I'm sorry, I can't imagine how that has happened, I can't help you anymore,' said Diogenes.

Professor Bi was busy typing away on two different computers seemingly enlivened by Diogenes's fruit lozenge. Diogenes left the laboratory and caught a taxi to the airport.

Diogenes was on board a plane heading for London without being treated like a fugitive due to his new CD status, and after some single malt in business class he was cleared right through to his London residence, before he dropped in to his literary agent Mordechai McIntyre. His cleaner had been sacked since she inadvertently diverted a manuscript into his rival's portfolio next door and the only concession to cleaning since that time had been air conditioning, and even that had become defunct due to being clogged with cannabis fumes.

'Long time no see, I've been meaning to get back to you,' said Mordechai.

'How can I help?' asked Diogenes.

'By bloody re-writing the whole lot of this stuff; no I jest, but this country music doll. How does she figure, I mean, I can't see how she comes into this story and how she links in with all this chemical stuff and the drugging of manic double agents?' asked the rather confused agent.

'Manic double agents, are you sure you have the right manuscript?' asked Diogenes.

'Well, what do I know, I am a simple scribe, and you are winding me up. No-one but you could serve up such stuff; you should see some of the other stuff I get with chic lit and crime dramas with more improbable detectives every day. Do you know one manuscript had a lead detective who was dead throughout the entire novel? And then there is the question I have been asking for some time,' said Mordechai.

'And what would that be? asked Diogenes.

'Is this science fiction?' asked Mordechai.

'Do you want me to test some of this out on you?' asked Diogenes.

Poor Mordechai, despite his arty-farty veneer, he was a realist at heart and he fished out some single malt for both of them to sample that had been donated by a grateful client. After a few shots they both became the best of friends again and they even hugged before Diogenes struggled through the heaps of manuscripts and crisp packets to some fresh air and a taxi to the college laboratory that served as a base.

His student Marie, who had been plucked from a prominent French university, looked extremely satisfied with Diogenes as a supervisor and was hanging on to his every word.

'The Volpowsky equation suited my needs just perfectly,' said Marie.

'I'm glad to hear that, but I really need you to demonstrate some initiative of your own now. Your work is moving in the right direction but we need some breakthroughs for that extra spurt that is going to make you an international voice,' said Diogenes.

'Are you saying that I am not good enough?' said Marie with damp eyes.

'No, I am not saying that, but how about you look to take this to another level. Maybe if you call me later I can explain,' said Diogenes.

Diogenes moved to an adjacent office with one of his senior colleagues and an elderly man in a suit.

'I think we met in Manchester,' said Leonardo.

'Yes, excellent venue. Has the season finished?' asked Diogenes.

'Their season may have finished but ours is only just starting,' said Leonardo.

'What do we have on the agenda?' asked Diogenes.

'Only one item I am afraid, but you have to get this right,' said Leonardo.

'And that is?' asked Diogenes.

'Suicide bombers,' said Leonardo. 'We need you out in Afghanistan to do some field work. This has become a real political hot potato and we feel that if there is someone who can find a solution, it is you.'

'I feel quite flattered but I am always up for a challenge. No doubt you have made the appropriate arrangements,' said Diogenes.

Leonardo handed him a briefcase.

'Everything you need should be in here. But it is not a challenge, it is an order. Our existence as a free nation depends on you,' said Leonardo.

Although he had not been back in London for long, he opened the envelope and flew to Afghanistan on a scheduled flight.

Diogenes had been allocated an office in Kabul, which from the outside resembled a butcher's shop, complete with portions of camel meat and chickens hanging on hooks outside. As he entered the shop, the butcher opened a door to reveal a steel and glass interior and a lift which the butcher operated by a key pad. On reaching the floor above, he was met by a civil servant who showed him to an office. He had been allocated a desk and a laptop and he began to programme his BlackBerry with the latest data. According to his instructions he had an arrangement to meet the health minister in his office. The life expectancy of a government minister in Afghanistan was under twelve months and so Diogenes was keen to get what he wanted quickly.

'I need some tissue from two suicide bombers, one successful one and one who failed,' said Diogenes.

'This will need clearance at the highest level. I will need at least a month for that alone,' said the minister.

'I need the tissue flown out to Geneva tomorrow so that I can get to work on the project,' said Diogenes.

Diogenes handed over his letters of authority to the minister, who was sweating much more than at the beginning of the meeting, and Diogenes organised a taxi to take him to a safe house in the suburbs, as per his instructions. The journey seemed to take a while and the driver was sweating and talking to himself.

'I think I had better get out here,' said Diogenes.

The driver turned round, having retrieved a pistol from the glove compartment, and sped off through dirt roads into the mountains, past lines of refugees with bundles of their worldly possessions balancing precariously on their backs. Diogenes felt as if his body was being gripped in a giant vice as a machine gun-toting paramilitary was waiting to greet him. His corner of a room was pointed out as he was supplied with a bottle of water and some fruit, along with some rather unappealing bed linen.

'What is all this about?' asked Diogenes.

A bunch of heavily-armed men were arguing about something and the tall one moved up to Diogenes with his bazooka.

'We want you get us money and the liberation of our comrades who are persecuted all over the Western world,' said the tall man.

'Is this the usual way of asking for help in these parts?' asked Diogenes.

The rest of the conversation took place in an amalgamation of languages but the demands did not seem to be less fervent. They had Mexican-style bandoliers and turbans which made them look as if they were part of a West End musical. Diogenes was wondering whether to be worried or sing, when a fat bandit pulled out a kukri and exclaimed 'Aoy Ghurkali'. He was no Ghurkha, but the proximity of his kukri to Diogenes's carotid artery was rather worrying.

8

Ingrid had a dilemma; she had been dragged into an international scenario at the highest level, which was way out of her league. This was not the first time she had faced challenges that were different, and she was always able to adapt to them, but not on this scale. Leadership was not her problem; she had always excelled at everything asked of her from when she was a just another kid and this was made more difficult by her father who was a dilettante and a mother who always made herself available to the sick. Despite this, her brother Inge and herself had learned to adapt, and the similarity of their name demonstrated how little interest their parents took in them. Indeed, if the family had been lower down the social scale, the children may have been taken into care.

Ingrid and Inge had climbed to the top of their chosen fields but it was the potential fallout from any mistakes that worried her. In her own mind, any major transgression would simply reinforce in her parents' minds that she was not worth the effort. T-Bone and his friends were working their way through the bar stocks and getting louder all the time. Their Stetsons and their singing made them stand out and there did not seem to be any end in sight.

'Are you serious about this revolution, T-Bone?' asked Sue.

'What makes you think I ain't?' said T-Bone.

'But there are millions of Americans and things are way more sophisticated than they were at the time of the civil war a hundred and fifty years ago, and you lost big time then,' said Sue.

'We got plenty of southern folk just raring to go and the south has all the money and what we ain't got now, we can find ways of getting, no fear,' said T-Bone.

'How many troops are we talking about, T-Bone?' asked Sue.

'How many you need?' asked T-Bone.

'C'mon, T-Bone, if we don't get the logistics right we are talking about another bloodbath,' said Sue.

'How's about five figures?' asked T-Bone.

'Five?' asked Sue.

'OK, six,' said T-Bone.

Sue was beginning to wonder whether all this talk was bullshit Confederate fantasy or reality. Zack the drummer joined in.

'We got training camps and all, and ev'ry Texan has his own arsenal at home from pistols to bazookas,' said Zack.

'Training camps?' asked Sue.

'Well, if Bin Laden can get 'em jumping over rocks in Pakistan, then I'm sure we can go one better than that, ma'am,' said Zack.

'How many of you are in the training camps?' asked Sue

'Well in the last camp at Baton Rouge we had over fifty thousand, all kitted up and ready to roll,' said T-Bone.

Sue looked at the Galveston Rebels in their Buckskins, at T-Bone and then at Chuck. Could she rely on this motley crew or was this just moonshine talking? Amongst all this bravado and sabre rattling, Sue suddenly remembered Freddie and his Egyptian emergency. It was better for her be in the present rather than the future and it was time for her to go back to being Ingrid so that she could get back to her ministerial role. She headed to Dulles airport in Washington DC before changing into her business suit and catching the first flight out to Cairo.

She landed in Cairo to be met by a ministerial

Mercedes and a uniformed chauffeur. Freddie was in the bar at the MOD accompanied by a few miscellaneous old-timers in uniforms with medal ribbons and caps with gold braid and gold badges full of Arabic mottoes and rich coloured symbols. They were ushered into the board room where the table was laden with alcohol and ashtrays, and the worried officials were trying to decide how to cope with the forthcoming disaster. Ingrid, as a member of the cabinet, arrived with a thick dossier of material for the meeting. She already had another folder with some contract details for an album that she had agreed to make and some case notes for some operations that she had been booked in to perform around the world. The prime minister stood up chatting with the rest of the room, except for Freddie, who was retrieving data.

'Welcome home, Ingrid. I hope you had a comfortable trip. We are sorry to present you with such a dilemma but we felt that we needed the benefit of your logistical skills before we made any decisions,' said the prime minister.

'How have you ended up with all these problems?' asked Ingrid.

'I think we made some assumptions that we were not entitled to make, and one or two of our more head-strong colleagues pushed things a little too far,' said the prime minister.

'Do you have control on the streets?' asked Freddie.

Freddie had paused from his electronic meanderings and peaked out of the window. Crowds were welling up with any weapon that was to hand and the police and army looked tense as they formed a barrier. Out of sight were arsenals of tear gas, rubber bullets, water cannons and live ammunition.

'How long do we have until it gets ugly and the United Nations begins to pass resolutions?' asked

Freddie.

'The UN doesn't really have any clout these days. Most of its resolutions are either ignored or opposed by other revolutionary regimes,' said the prime minister. 'Do you have anything for us Ingrid?'

'I might do, depending on whether you want any outside help,' said Ingrid.

'We desperately need something as it is getting to boiling point here, as you can see,' said the prime minister.

'How do you feel about a foreign militia supporting your forces?' asked Ingrid.

'If you can discuss this with Freddie it would be a great help, Ingrid,' said the prime minister.

Ingrid and Freddie relocated to Freddie's office which was in the same building and appeared to be a blend of the colonial past and a disaster area. The furniture was antique and in need of extensive restoration and the walls were open to the elements where the locals had vented their feelings on the ruling system by firing mortar bombs and grenades. Freddie rang a bell and tea and pastries appeared carried on a large tray by a small man with a fez.

'Am I glad to see you Ingrid,' said Freddie.

'You've only been here a few minutes and it's a disaster area. What have you been doing?' asked Ingrid.

'Don't look at me. You can see that I hardly had time to move in and get to know the place when all this lot outside started kicking off and demanding solutions to problems,' said Freddie.

'Look Freddie, I am just a humble surgeon, so I am probably more out of my depth than anyone here,' said Ingrid.

'Who are this secret army that are going to be jetted in to help?' asked Freddie.

'Let me just pass this by you. I have just returned from the US and there appears to be a groundswell of opinion in the south that they are being sold out by the Yankees. A throwback to the civil war if you like,' said Ingrid.

'You're not expecting us to start marching for Dixie, are you?' asked Freddie.

'Not exactly, but they could be marching for us,' said Ingrid.

'You mean a whole regiment of Confederate militia can be shipped out here to police the place?' asked Freddie.

'Not only to police it, we could also use their organisational knowhow, and the weather would be no problem for them; indeed it would be a break from the hurricanes and tornados out here,' said Ingrid.

'Interesting, but who will lead all of this and how does it fit in with the Egyptians who have been here for millennia?' asked Freddie.

'That's where you come in Freddie. With your contacts in higher places, I am sure that we will be able to set up a civil service over here with international links,' said Ingrid.

'Yes I'm sure that will be no problem; it will just take a few minutes,' said Freddie with some sarcasm.

Freddie pressed a button on his BlackBerry and showed it to Ingrid. It read "you are requested to meet Yossi in the Neurosurgical unit in Haifa, it is an emergency."

'Did you know about this Freddie?'

'I had inkling. But I think you may need this.'

Freddie produced a small plastic tub marked "sterile and toxic" and handed it to Ingrid. She made some enquiries at the office of the chief of civil service about transportation to Israel and she was fixed up with a Turkish Airlines flight to Tel Aviv.

Ingrid had moved quickly from war-torn Cairo to Haifa using her newly-acquired CD status and was ushered to a private suite in the neurosurgical unit, reserved for the Drohobyczerrebbe. Apart from the man himself, the walls were lined with black coated ultra-orthodox Jews facing east and swaying in a regular fashion as they read or chanted prayers. The rebbe was attached to a life-support system and was covered with amulets and folded up parchment containing bits of prayer, to speed recovery. Yossi was the head of the unit, and a highly regarded surgeon in his own right, and he led Ingrid to one of his offices.

'What is happening in there?' asked Ingrid.

'In there you see the Drohobyczerrebbe. He comes from a long dynasty of Talmudic scholars going back to the fifteenth century in Eastern Europe. The current rebbe has no male heirs and his wife died in the same attack that injured him, but there is a nubile girl lined up for him, if he survives. So the line that has existed for several hundred years depends on him surviving and there are thousands of his followers, all over the world, who hold on to his every word,' said Yossi.

'So what happened to him?' asked Ingrid.

'Hamas set up an ambush for the IDF, but unfortunately the rebbe was passing by on the way home from teaching some disciples and as he came into sight there was a firefight and he took a bullet in the brain,' said Yossi.

'I presume you have scans here,' said Ingrid.

'There are no shortage of scans, as the sect has numerous donations from all over the world, and the rebbe and his followers have sole control over the spending,' said Yossi.

Yossi ushered Ingrid into a clinical room full of screens which not only showed the bullet, but also the track it took before it lodged in its final resting place. It was like viewing the trail left by a rocket in its wake, only this was not the sky, it was damaged brain tissue. The usual treatment of brain damage was simply to wait and see, and even the removal of the bullet was not without risk, as it might kill the patient or leave him severely brain-damaged. Ingrid followed the signs to the operating suite as the praying men moved aside.

The operating theatre was state of the art, but the religious contingent was confined to the multi-faith room, for hygiene reasons. Ingrid met the team It was obvious that the damage and the scarring were extensive, and even after the bullet had been removed and put in a dish for the ballistic people, the work had only just begun. Ingrid put Freddie's tub on to a tray and unravelled the mesh inside. As Ingrid cleansed and removed debris, she could see missing pieces of brain and was stemming the bleeding. Then she removed the mesh from the tub and laid it along the damaged areas, before securing it with adhesive paste.

'What is this Ingrid?' asked Yossi.

'Just something a friend knocked together. It will generate nerve growth through the receptors,' said Ingrid as she checked that she had not left any gaps.

'But this has never even been written up,' said Yossi.

'Cutting edge, my dear, cutting edge. Don't worry, all is in hand,' said Ingrid reassuringly.

Ingrid left the rest of the staff to tidy up and close the wound, whilst she wrote her notes and texted Freddie. He texted her to tell her that there were ten companies of men flying from Dallas to Cairo and five of his diplomatic friends were already in the area, and would join him presently. He also reassured Ingrid that he had tried the mesh on twenty rabbits, and the preliminary findings were promising. Ingrid helped herself to some Israeli liquor and experienced tension for the first time in a few years. Even Yossi joined the team in prayer to the success of a possible world first brain repair procedure. Ingrid preferred to use the alcohol instead.

After a cordon bleu kosher experience in the most expensive restaurant in town, courtesy of the Israeli Ministry of Health, they went back to the ward to review the patient. The room had been cleared of the religious contingent and was just an intensive care facility with tubes and monitors. Yossi enquired after the patient.

'Well he is breathing and noticing things which is quite amazing considering the previous few weeks,' said the nurse in charge.

Ingrid smiled and checked his limbs and his pupils.

'OK, I think I have done all that I can here. Do keep in touch and I am sure that the doctors here will not hesitate to get in touch if needs be, can someone get me to the airport in Tel Aviv please?' asked Ingrid.

Another text arrived from Freddie, "we are ready to roll and we have control of the place now, hope your patient survives."

9

His captors were dressed in an odd mixture of military style uniforms and Diogenes thought he spotted a soviet admiral, but he soon came to realise that the clothing had been recycled from the dead. He realised that even his clothes may soon be recycled when he saw the kukri-wielding gangster.

'I have something for you, that's why I am here, if you let me, then I will tell you,' Diogenes said in a shaky voice. He was not used to having his life threatened in such close proximity and he was fearful that one wrong move could signal the end for him.

The group of gangsters noticed that their comrade with a kukri had bloodshot eyes, with his hand shaking, and could be about to destroy their valuable commodity. The leader with a shaven head strode over and grabbed the wrist of the man with the kukri and twisted it until there was a click, at which the blade dropped and the attacker screeched, causing his helmet to drop on to his assailant. The leader then lifted him off the ground and flung him into a wall.

'What have we told you about making noises? I had my doubts about bringing you and if it wasn't for your sister you would still be in the institution. What is this you have for us mister?' shouted the leader as he picked up the kukri and kicked the previous assailant.

'Have you never thought what a Westerner might be doing here?' asked Diogenes.

'We have our ideas, but we need some money and that is why you are still alive,' said the leader.

'Well I can't help you with that but I think that killing me would not be a smart move,' said Diogenes as he wiped the sweat from his forehead. He could feel one of his pains coming on and he wondered whether they had any whiskey.

'Not a smart move, ha, that doesn't matter to us, you are just another one, and there will be more in the future, so you do not have long to get us what we want,' said the leader laughing.

'What exactly do you want from me?' asked Diogenes. 'And how do you expect me to do anything when some of you don't seem to be able to control yourselves.'

'Let me worry about that, you just do what we tell you,' said the leader.

'Well, it is in your interest to keep me alive otherwise no-one will pay anything for me and there will be reprisals and not only you, but many of your friends will perish,' said Diogenes having recovered his composure.

'We are not going to be blackmailed and we don't need anything, but, if you want to help us, you go ahead, but we do not trust anyone and particularly someone who is white because we can supply all the action,' said the leader.

The leader rejoined the group as the man without the kukri lay where he had been deposited, gripping his rather deformed wrist and moaning. Diogenes found his BlackBerry and he was pleased to see that the material that he had requested had been emailed to him. He engaged the app that was labelled biogenic calculations and began to move around various symbols and figures. It wasn't long before the leader noticed this and grabbed the BlackBerry.

'You are making calls to your friends who will come to kill us,' he said.

'I can assure you that I was not. I would not be that stupid, you can check it if you like,' said Diogenes.

'This is something in your own language and you think that I am stupid not to know this. You insult me and my comrades. You give me a reason why I should not kill you?' shouted the leader.

'Do you want to know about bomb making?' asked Diogenes.

'What can you tell us about this? We are pretty good already, look how many NATO people we eliminate daily; you can read it in the papers or watch on CNN or Al Jazeera,' sneered the leader.

'Maybe, but how many men do you lose when things don't go right? You can see that on CNN as well. Is it worth sending suicide bombers and then all the reprisals that kill your people and set back your cause?' asked Diogenes.

'You have a better idea?' asked the leader.

'Well try me out and if I have, then let me go,' said Diogenes.

'And if you haven't?'

'I think you know what to do,' said Diogenes.

'They think that you are Jewish,' said the leader.

'What do you want me to do about that?' asked Diogenes.

'Something a bit personal,' said the leader with uncharacteristic coyness.

Diogenes obliged; there was no scar from the Geneva day surgery and it was enough to satisfy the leader. Instead of arguments there were smiles and nods, and drinks were poured as the contents of paper bags were eaten. When Diogenes saw this he sampled his food and, although it looked like something even an animal would leave behind, he decided that his hunger needed some solution and he washed it down with the water, wishing it was whiskey.

'What is it that you have for us?' asked the leader.

'I will need the data on my BlackBerry that you have taken.'

'How do I know that you will not use it to call for

help?' asked the leader.

'What is the point of me doing that? If I do I will be killed along with you, so it does not help me. I have not come here to volunteer to be a suicide bomber,' said Diogenes impatiently as he realised he was dealing with fools.

'We can volunteer you to be a suicide bomber,' said the leader impatiently.

'I am well aware of that.'

Diogenes resumed calculations on his BlackBerry whilst the group produced some playing cards and busied themselves with gambling to relieve the boredom. They threw the injured Ghurkha impersonator a porn magazine, but the limited use of his hand rather took the shine off that treat. The group laughed and began to relax, except for the leader, who simply sat and cleaned his weapon.

'I need you to get me some ingredients for this. Can you give me some paper and a pen and I will make a list?' asked Diogenes.

One of the group members set off in a battered old Fiat with the list to threaten some shopkeepers in the local village. Diogenes resumed his calculations as some of the group slept whilst others strolled outside for some fresh air and to check on the status of anybody who might be threatening them. The terrain was rocky and void of any sign of life as even the animals and plants had abandoned it. The man with the shopping soon arrived and it was deposited next to the man who had been designated as a bomb maker. He was a small wiry man with short stubby fingers and a thumb missing on each hand. He wore thick glasses that were cracked and almost opaque.

'I think we had better go outside for this so that the mountain does not come down on top of us,' said Diogenes.

'What have you got for me?' asked the bomb maker with a French accent.

'OK, just put it on the ground and you will need some containers and a stick to mix up the ingredients,' said Diogenes in an authoritative manner.

The bomb maker worked tirelessly examining the labels through his damaged spectacles. Diogenes talked him through it in a vague manner whilst the leader sat and watched and kept an eye out for anything suspicious.

'Why is this anything different from what we all use every day? The ingredients are a little different but at the end of the day we just want to kill as many people as possible,' said the bomb maker suspiciously.

'This is very different and I can guarantee that it is more than double the efficiency,' said Diogenes.

'Our recipe is based on the Al-Khatum system but you are using more of some ingredients and you are using less, or even none, of others, and there are items like nutmeg and baking soda that we do not use,' said the bomb maker.

'I thought you would spot that, but I am utilising the nutmeg for the myristicin and the elemicin, which accelerates the reaction, and the baking soda to stabilise the acid elements,' said Diogenes with a degree of authority that came from years of practising real science.

The leader looked puzzled but smiled as any demonstration of ignorance usually revealed weakness. The chemical mixing was going well and Diogenes had a quick look and a smell, like a sommelier, and he nodded in approval.

'Just put the solution behind that rock over there and wait whilst I complete my calculations,' said Diogenes with a degree of authority.

'Where do you want us to stand?' asked the leader.

'Just stand near me so if it fails or goes wrong, that is your guarantee of my credentials,' said Diogenes.

Diogenes moved a few apps around on his BlackBerry, nodded, and looked at the container before retreating to the others as he pressed the green button. There wasn't so much as a bang; it was more of a loud fizzing like before a firework went off as the group began to stiffen up and slither to the floor with contorted faces. There was a strong smell of burning but the bomb appeared to be unexploded and was still intact. Diogenes examined the bodies of the group and found the usual burnt-out eye sockets, but he noticed that a few of them had a profuse flow of clear fluid coming down their noses. He left them lifeless and commandeered their Fiat, looking for a village. After several kilometres of rubble and the remains of freedom fighters, he realised he was at risk of another embarrassing episode and so he stopped off the beaten track and texted the health minister with his GPS data and before long he was transported in a USA armoured vehicle back to the government office that he had recently left.

After a swift debrief he requested some video-conferencing facilities and a US technician.

'Where do you want to video conference to, sir?' asked the US army corporal in his camouflage fatigues.

'I think the details are here on this BlackBerry, I will ring them to give warning of my contact, corporal,' said Diogenes.

Diogenes found a whiteboard and some coloured pens and completed his equations as the technician fiddled with the equipment.

'Are we ready to roll sir, have you finished with that science on the whiteboard?' said the corporal.

'Yes we are, I have cleared it to go through now,' said Diogenes.

The health minister and one of his scientific advisers were on line.

'Diogenes, what have you got for us?' asked the health minister.

'Well it is not much but there is a lot more scientific data and I need to be at the laboratories to develop these ideas a little more,' said Diogenes.

'Do you want us to get you back to Geneva, now?' asked the minister.

'Not at the moment, as I haven't even started what I set off to do,' said Diogenes.

'How's about we send Mamser to collect your stuff in a diplomatic bag, have you any instructions?' asked the minister.

'Yes I want a paper bag analysed by Professor Bi. It is soaked in the fluid from a couple of deceased gentlemen who I will tell you about at some later date. If you can also mention nutmeg with alkaline contamination along with myristicin and elemicin, that would be excellent,' said Diogenes.

'We will indeed, I don't pretend to know what you are talking about but I trust that you know best,' said the minister.

'Oh and also can you pass my compliments to the surgeon in Geneva and tell him the operation worked a treat,' said Diogenes.

10

Freddie had been allocated the presidential suite in a state of the art hotel in Cairo, within walking distance from the airport. Ingrid was sipping the house cocktail from a glass the shape of the sphinx. Freddie was fondling his way round the various inlets that constituted the smooth contours of her body, like a relief map. He was muscular as well as being enormous and he was no slouch in manoeuvring his way round her pert breasts and her thighs that had been softened by extra-virgin olive oil. She was used to attention and seemed to know his anatomy like she knew her surgery. The foreplay was focussed and they played each other's bodies like members of an orchestra. The timing was perfect and they were able to hold the top note as if there had been a conductor present. Air conditioning made sure they were not inconvenienced by the elements.

After their amorous interlude, Ingrid and Freddie relocated to his office in the Ministry of Defence.

'How did that operation go, is the rebbe still alive?' asked Freddie.

'Still alive, do you doubt my skills?' said Ingrid impatiently.

'Indeed no, my dear, on the contrary, there is no-one better. It was my own skills that I was calling into question,' said Freddie on the defence. He was used to her prickly side, indeed it turned him on.

'Well you will be happy to know he was already coming round as I left, so I think your rabbit mesh might be of some use,' said Ingrid in triumph.

'We think some of the rabbits may have contracted myxomatosis, but not to worry,' said Freddie scratching his head.

'Not to worry, doesn't it make you twitch and salivate?' said Ingrid, with some concern.

'Only in a pop song by Radiohead,' quipped Freddie.

'So what have you organised over here in my absence?' asked Ingrid.

'Oh we've got the whole country under control now. Your Confederate friends have set up a militia and the elements of an invasion force. My friends have set up a civil service and I have appointed a new Minister of Science, a boxing mate of mine and a great boffin called Issy Schlumberger,' said Freddie.

'You don't hang about do you Freddie, you've set up a whole country in a few days. Some places take centuries and still don't get it right,' laughed Ingrid.

'Oh I am not saying I've got it right, but it will do for the moment, while we clear up the mess that everyone else left behind. Oh yes, you don't know where I can get an academic library do you?' asked Freddie.

Ingrid was receiving a text message.

"Drohobyczerrebbe is walking and talking and thousands of his disciples think you are the Messiah, please confirm that you aren't, if appropriate. Tamuz."

Ingrid smiled.

'I'm not sure about the library, Freddie, what's in it for me if I can get you one?'

'I think I need to introduce you to some of the personnel involved in running our new country, so I have arranged for them to be gathered in a place down the road, but I need to be appropriately dressed,' said Freddie.

A ministerial Mercedes delivered Ingrid and Freddie to one of the few grand buildings still standing in Cairo and, after ritual salutes from guards, a tall man with a Texan drawl greeted them.

'I would like to introduce the Minister of Health who is working closely with us in Operation Renaissance,' said Freddie.

'I am pleased to be of assistance gentlemen,' said the Texan. 'It is difficult for Ingrid, the Minister of Health, to remember all the names so I have prepared a leaflet to detail the staff, and their backgrounds, and I am sure in time you will be able to gel together'.

'I will look forward to that,' said Ingrid with some trepidation.

Ingrid thumbed her way through the leaflet as a group of middle-aged to elderly gentlemen were introduced. Most of them had acquired either awards at all levels up to the Knighthood. The exceptions were professors or high-ranking military types, but nobility were also in the mix, in deference to Freddie's blood line. Freddie put his feet upon the desk and fiddled with his electronic devices. He had reproduced his science laboratory in the centre of Cairo and had made himself at home as much as he had in numerous other places in the past. Often he had just moved on out of frustration with the demands of his hosts but occasionally the odd experiment had gone wrong and he had thought it prudent to relocate rapidly to avoid embarrassing questions. As Ingrid rose to leave, the building began to shudder and its previous impregnability was cast in doubt as a portion of Freddie's office crumbled and sank. There was dust everywhere and some black acrid smoke rose outside as sirens rang and the sound of screaming and barked orders became apparent. As they picked their way through the rubble, helmeted security officers channelled survivors to a grass square in the middle of a large quadrangle. The fire chief approached Freddie.

'It looks like a single bomb but there was no car or other vehicle, sir.'

'Are we talking of a suicide bomber?' asked Freddie.

'It's difficult to say, but there are reports of person wearing a burkha seen just before the explosion,' explained the fire chief.

'Can you take me to the source of the explosion and get someone to bring a receptacle and a trowel?' asked Freddie.

Amongst the chaos and debris there was one spot that was splattered with human remains and black fabric remnants. Freddie scraped up all that he could and directed one of the staff to bag it up and keep it secure. The advantage of the recent change in regime was that there was no need to request foreign aid; a US style rescue service and an international logistic team acted to minimise the collateral damage. Ingrid had found a conference room where she had assembled the civil servants for a debrief. Issy Schlumberger and the rather odd collection of gentlemen brought their coffee to the table along with a notepad. Issy had enjoyed an unparalleled reputation bridging the gap between every day events and pure science. He had coined the word logo-technics for his speciality and although he was now well into his eighth decade he was still called upon to help all manner of problems. Issy opened the conversation:

'We need to find out where this is coming from and why it is happening. It can't be a protest as we haven't even begun to legislate properly or make any decisions, so there is nothing to protest about.'

'Do you think he was an Islamic fundamentalist?' asked Ingrid.

'I think he was mentally deranged whatever calling he professed to have,' said Issy. 'And we need a way to tap into what is going on out there.'

Ingrid was scrolling through her BlackBerry for

some ideas and a text message came up:

"Ingrid, long time no see, how far up the ladder have you climbed, Carlo x".

She texted back:

"Too far, Carlo, Ingrid x".

"Can I help?" texted Carlo.

"Of course you can, can you get yourself to Cairo, ASAP?" texted Ingrid.

The presidential palace had kitted out its banquet suite for Carlo's arrival and a bulletproof car brought him round the heaps of rubble and old ordinance. At every block was a Confederate soldier with a rather lethal looking machine gun and a walkie-talkie as well as several bandoliers of bullets that could pierce anything and anyone. In the middle of this, life went on as bazaars and the roadside cafes served Turkish coffee with hookahs bubbling, customers chewing betel nuts, and spitting. There was chaos but there had always been chaos, and this was just different chaos. Carlo, in his white suit, was ushered into the only room with air conditioning that worked. Ingrid met him in an anti-room to set the scene.

'Don't ask how, but I am the Minister of Health here and, along with an old friend, you remember Freddie, we are running the place.'

'You still have the same radiance, my dear, as ever. I never did like Freddie you know, but let's let bygones etc.'

'Time moves on Carlo, and at the moment we need anyone who can help,'

'I hope I'm not anyone,' said Carlo.

'Carlo, you are always special, as you know,' said Ingrid.

'OK, OK, OK, sorry I'm listening,' said Carlo.

'Let's join the others,' said Ingrid.

'Must we?' asked Carlo sensing that their intimate

tet a tet was coming to an end.

'Carlo!' smiled Ingrid.

The room was jammed with Confederate army chiefs, a collection of boffins from round the world as well as diplomats, royalty and political movers and shakers. Issy, newly-elected Minister of Science, outlined the problem.

'We are pleased to welcome you to the Confederate State of Egypt, Carlo. As you may have noticed, we appear to be in the middle of an insurrection and, despite the imposition of law and order and some sound government, this does not seem to be controlling matters. I am not sure whether you can help, but Ingrid here assures us that you are a fixer like no other,' said Issy.

'I had better outline my credentials for this task before we go much further, to see whether I fit the bill. I have been a US congressman for more years than I can remember, and have been at the centre of government through many crises from the Cuban missile stand-off via Vietnam and into the Middle-Eastern problems and post nine eleven. Before politics I originate from a Georgia family with Italian origins. I graduated from Harvard and then became a movie director before I moved into politics,' explained Carlo.

'That sounds as if you would fit in superbly to our group, but do you think you can help us?' asked Issy.

'Well I can't personally, but I know a man who can, and I have arranged for him to be here tomorrow. He is called Massimo Di Palermo and he has helped me a great deal over the years,' replied Carlo.

'And what is his background?' asked Issy.

'He was a liaison officer working for the FBI and linking with the CIA,' explained Carlo.

'Will you be working with him?' asked Issy.

'Well I only have a window for a few days and then

I have some business in Europe, so I will make sure he is bedded in before I leave if that is what you want,' said Carlo.

The meeting split up and Freddie and Ingrid moved across the road to the Café Morocco, and the smell of tobacco together with the Turkish coffee was a test of your lung function to manage more than five minutes. The locals would spend all day there, as work was traditionally part-time in Cairo.

'Ingrid, I vaguely remember Carlo but I can't quite place him, he seems to have all the contacts anyone needs,' said Freddie.

'Your memory is deteriorating; it must be all those gases you use in the lab. You once fought a duel with him,' said Ingrid.

'And did I win?' asked Freddie.

'Well yes, but that's a long story, I'll tell you some other time, but suffice to say I haven't seen him for a few years, you'll see.'

11

After some discussion the minister arranged for the British high command to collaborate with Diogenes so as to minimise any future complications. An extremely large armoured vehicle with what looked like a regiment of heavily armoured outriders arrived as Diogenes was squeezed in between several large troopers. Although Diogenes was fit and strong, he was about half the weight of his escorts and the constriction around his body was making his asthma come on. Diogenes waited outside Camp Bastion for an appointment with one of the British officers. His identification papers were sent through for the office staff to scrutinise and he was asked to stand by the main gate whilst the guards rested in an air-conditioned booth. The sand was so hot that his trainers smelt of molten rubber and he wondered how long it would be before he went the same way. A sergeant ambled out in camouflage dress and a green beret and pointed to Diogenes's papers as if he were touching something verminous. He unfastened the gun in his holster as he approached and motioned for some of his team to come forward.

'The major says that he has no knowledge of this and, looking at these papers, I don't think you would be welcome in here,' said the sergeant, as he returned the papers to Diogenes.

Diogenes examined the papers and immediately noticed that they indicated that he was a Syrian fruit seller, and the passport was full of evidence of extensive Middle-East travel. He put his hand in his pocket and the sergeant's hand moved closer to his pistol.

'Look I am sorry sergeant, let me explain. In my

work I have to carry a variety of papers and I inadvertently gave you the wrong ones. You can search me, I am not armed, but the other papers are in my other pocket,' said Diogenes.

The sergeant frisked him, emptied his pocket, asked him to lie face down on the sand with his arms outspread and he put his military boot in the small of his back. He read through the other documents and noticed the CD stamp on them with links to the CIA and MI6. He left Diogenes spread-eagled on the baking sand with a corporal in close attendance while he set off again. As he lay there, Diogenes noticed squads of soldiers marching up and down, creating clouds of sand as someone shouted orders, but nobody seemed to notice him as he started wheezing and coughing. Before long a small thin soldier came up and hauled him to his feet. From his insignia on his camouflage Diogenes could see that he was a lieutenant, and after an apology he escorted Diogenes into Camp Bastion.

Diogenes was deposited into the tent/office of Major Marchbanks-Smith-Marchbanks who scrutinised his dishevelled appearance and the sand coming out of his jeans.

'Have you walked here from Kabul?' asked the major.

'No I was given a shake down by your sergeant at the front gate for daring to ask to meet you,' said Diogenes.

'I see, well we can't be too careful here you know; we don't want one of these suicide bomber chappies just wandering in,' said the major.

'I see, well I don't know how much you have been told, but I am after a couple of favours from you,' said Diogenes.

'Well fire away old chap, I'll see if we can help. Oh by the way I am the engineering man round here, the only one who has a maths O-level, so that may be of some help,' said the major.

'OK, I need some access to a defused IED and I also need to see a failed suicide bomber,' announced Diogenes.

'Rather an odd mixture if I may say, can you tell me what you want with them? Oh I'm sorry, I suppose it's classified and all that,' said the major looking confused.

'It is. Can you help?' asked Diogenes.

'Well, as for the suicide bomber, we wouldn't keep one of them here even if we had caught him. Too much security and all that. He, or indeed she, would be moved on by the coalition forces to an unknown destiny. As for the IED, we have a number of those, but I am not sure whether I can let you loose on them. Do you have any letters of authority?' asked the major.

The major's phone rang and after a few words he suddenly went pale with a green tinge and he began to sweat and shake.

'Look my friend, I am afraid we have an emergency here and I have been ordered to muster by the gold commander in the military hospital. I will leave you with my sergeant, Lucy, and she will keep you posted,' said the major in some haste as he sprinted towards some offices.

Lucy was an example of why thousands of rather shiftless boys back at home can't wait to join up. She was a slim peroxide blonde with the smallest bottom ever described, and a top that would never fit in a uniform, and so most of the buttons had to be left open to prevent her going into respiratory arrest. She even had some medal ribbons that rather matched her lip gloss. She was posing on her typist's chair in front of a screensaver of semi-clad male soldiers, with her uniform skirt in the form of a pelmet just below her crotch. She smiled at Diogenes as she played with her iPod smiling and laughing. A poster behind her was an army recruitment poster with a dizzy blonde beckoning the boys to join up. It didn't take much imagination to notice who was the poster girl. Diogenes was staring at the poster as he waited and fiddled with his BlackBerry. Lucy broke the silence:

'Are you thinking of joining up darling? You can have a signed one of those if you like,' she said smiling as she handed him a poster.

'It is tempting, I can see, but I'm here on a scientific visit so I have to decline but I can see why others would say yes,' said Diogenes with some regret.

'Oh I love soldiers, they are so strong and masterful, but I haven't met a scientist before, it must be so interesting,' said Lucy, as her pupils dilated.

'I wouldn't say that. We live in laboratories, generally wear white coats and fill computers and whiteboards with gobbledegook,' said Diogenes with even more regret.

'Lavatories?' asked Lucy suggestively.

'Laboratories,' said Diogenes smiling.

'Oh I am so silly sometimes. I just sit here and meet and greet people like you. But you don't look like a scientist; you look more like a suicide bomber. Oh I am so sorry, that is rude,' said Lucy flirtingly.

'Oh don't worry, most people say that; it's just that I do a lot of work with the military,' said Diogenes.

'The major is very nervous about the violence, you know. He sends me to sort all these types out, but it doesn't bother me you see, my father was a murderer, so I was brought up with it. I don't know how he'll cope with this suicide bomber in the hospital,' said Lucy.

'Suicide bomber,' said Diogenes as his pupils dilated.

'Oh, maybe I shouldn't have said that, me and my

mouth, my dad used to say that someone would do me in for that one day and he would know,' said Lucy smiling.

'Well Lucy, I can help here, that is what I do. Can you get them to take me there,' suggested Diogenes.

'Oh how sexy, I'll get on to the commanding officer PDQ,' said Lucy as she picked up her phone.

Within minutes two soldiers in full combat gear, bristling with weapons, marched up to Diogenes and handed him a flack-jacket with a helmet. After passing through several locked doors with sentries, they arrived at a large compound with a red cross on the door.

Diogenes was delivered to an armed response squad who were with the gold commander, and a rather portly Arab, in a mix and match military uniform, was standing near the patients in the hospital. He was talking in Arabic at a rapid rate and the interpreter was struggling to keep up.

'He is saying he is not afraid to die and the more of us he takes with him the better. He says that he has been sent on this mission as an honour to his tribe, and he looks forward to enjoying the virgins he will be allocated when he dies. He says his comrades have already made a video and it will be sent to Al Jazeera. He says that he is ready to be martyred, or something like that,' said the interpreter.

Diogenes fished out his BlackBerry and selected the appropriate icon and pressed the green button which had the effect of paralysing the bomber. Diogenes nodded to the assembled soldiers and smiled.

'What are you waiting for? Get all his paraphernalia off him, strip him naked, including his three pairs of underpants, and get a medic to search his orifices,' said Diogenes with an air of satisfaction.

'What have you done?' asked the gold commander.

'Just a little favour for you,' retorted Diogenes,

putting away his BlackBerry.

'But what are we to do with him now? How long will he stay like this?' asked the incredulous gold commander.

'I'm sorry I don't have that information. Classified, you understand, but I would plan for the long haul,' said Diogenes as he removed his heavy armoured clothing to the consternation of the soldiers.

The ordinance corps carefully placed the explosives in reinforced containers as the bomber was transported by stretcher to the detention suite, quite stiff, but breathing and with the same ecstatic expression as when he was in prayer. Diogenes was escorted back to Lucy who had heard it all via the gossip icon on her iPod. Lucy could not hide her excitement as she watched Diogenes dusting himself off.

'Oh how exciting, just pressing a few buttons on your BlackBerry. I think I'd like one of those. Where do you get yours?' she asked, as she made him a coffee.

'It takes years Lucy, but I'll show you one day; you don't have any single malt do you?' asked Diogenes, as his neck muscles tightened.

'I'd bet you would, and I'd like you to show me. What about when you're done here, I know a place where I can find some single malt, would you like to me to take you?'

As they were about to leave Major Marchbanks-Smith-Marchbanks strode in with his swagger stick and his gun.

'Well old boy, that was something special. I suppose I had no option but to give you what you wanted. Lucy here will take you to the ordinance room so that you can play with the IEDs and you can do what you want with your friend the bomber for a few days, until we can muster some RAF transport to ship him off,' announced the major.

'Well that's most generous of you major, but I don't think our bomber friend is going to be much use to me,' said Diogenes.

'I see, can you let me in on that, old boy?' said the major.

'Of course, you see I have just whacked out all the glutamate receptors in his mid-brain and the results could not be of any use because of that. But thanks anyway,' explained Diogenes to the bewildered soldier.

'And you can't tell us how long he is going to be like this. Is he safe to transport and how do we feed him etc?' asked the major.

'We don't have the data to tell when or whether he'll come out of this, so you will just have to play it by ear,' explained Diogenes.

'I see, very clever. I'll have to think about that, and how about feeding him?' asked the major.

'Well again it depends whether that is the road you want to go down, because if you get your medics to do that, you could be in for a long stretch with an individual who will spend all his life locked up. That has resource implications because if you start looking after him then you can't stop otherwise you will have lawyers and civil rights activists on your back. I could have killed him, but I needed to be sure that he couldn't move,' explained Diogenes.

'I see, but we don't keep them here, we just arrange for the RAF to get rid of them,' explained the major.

'You mean rendition?' asked Diogenes.

'Well I don't know anything about that. It is all further up the chain and I think my chain level is pretty low and I am too old to be able to climb any further,' explained the major.

'Do you think I could accompany my man on the RAF plane so that I can get access to those already in captivity? It's very important or I wouldn't ask,' begged Diogenes.

'Leave it with me my friend. Lucy, can you take our friend to ordinance, you know the way, and bring him back when he's finished?' ordered the major.

'Of course sir,' replied Lucy with a broad grin.

Diogenes followed Lucy through a warren of tunnels with no names or numbers on the doors. It was no longer than minutes before Lucy flung open a door and announced that they were stopping off for some refreshments first. As she tugged at the silver buttons on her tunic, her breasts almost sighed as if they had been liberated, and she turned to enable Diogenes to help her unclasp her white lace see-through bra to reveal scarlet erect nipples. She undid his jeans as she pulled up her skirt to a level just beneath her breasts as they stood to attention like guardsmen on parade. Her thong barely covered anything as she held tightly on to Diogenes as he stepped out of his clothes. The bed in the corner was spotless and she deposited her key in her tunic pocket before guiding Diogenes into a blissful world of Lucyness. They had both needed this break as they exploded into each other and for Diogenes it more than compensated for his need for single malt. Whatever Diogenes gave, Lucy wanted more and it seemed like an age before they were able to make it to the ordinance room. Diogenes had to concentrate before he found what he wanted and he dismantled a few devices and took samples which he deposited in containers which he labelled and slipped into an army kitbag. After about ten minutes he pronounced himself satisfied and Lucy led him off.

'Won't they wonder where we've been?' asked Diogenes.

'Oh no, they are used to me going walk-about. We could go back for a bit more if you like. I never like leaving a man in need,' said Lucy as she adjusted her hair and makeup.

'My god Lucy, you are something special, but I think we both need some rest, don't you?' remarked Diogenes.

'Oh no, not me. I can carry on for hours. I just love it, especially with a real life hero. What about that BlackBerry?' asked Lucy.

'You are a BlackBerry, Lucy. When I come back I will show you how to do some special things with your iPad,' said Diogenes, smiling.

'Ooh I bet you will!' laughed Lucy.

Lucy made a call and one of the orderlies came in to escort Diogenes back to the major as Lucy blew a kiss after him. The major was sitting in his leather chair signing orders and transferring them from one tray to another.

'I hope you got what you wanted,' said the major.

'Most definitely, sir, and the RAF flight?' asked Diogenes.

'Tomorrow at 0400 hours or you'll miss it,' said the major checking in his diary.

'Excellent, sir, I will be there,' replied Diogenes.

12

Ingrid's phone rang: this time it was Saudi Arabia and apparently yet another intractable case, and it was a royal prince. It was touch and go whether he would survive and due to the enormous amount of petrodollars involved they were willing to do anything to save him. They had arranged for Ingrid to fly first class that afternoon to Jeddah.

Ingrid was transported to her destination in a royal car with outriders and taken through spotless empty corridors where she was invited to sit in the clinical diagnostics room in the royal suite at the international hospital. She noticed that, in another room, the regular doctors were clad in spotless white gowns looking anxious and hopeless at the same time. It was quite possible that their livelihood depended on the prognosis of this patient. On two walls were electronic screens attached to cables linked to the patient's body and the other wall had hand-wash facilities and sterile gowns. There was a lounge area just off the main room where the patient's wives and children were crying and praying. Ingrid scrolled through the data on the screens and checked the test results as the local professional team looked on and she could see out of the corner of her eye that they were whispering to each other and arguing about whether they would be in trouble for forgetting to do something.

'He is going to need me to go in but his condition is grave and most surgeons would not touch him due to the risk of death, what do you want me to do?' Ingrid asked the surgeons. She knew the answer to this but she always liked to leave people in no doubt as to her intentions. The family were in a huddle in the next room fingering their worry beads as they shook their heads in desperation for some divine intervention. Meanwhile Ingrid texted Freddie with her requirements as if she was getting in the weekly shopping from the grocers.

After the preliminary scrubbing, she opened the royal patient's skull and, with the use of suction, she could see a leak in the cranial vessels, and more importantly, the damage to the brain caused by the resulting loss of oxygen. In his case the damage was localised to one brain area rather than a more generalised type, similar to what she had found in the rebbe's case. She cleared the debris; it was just a case of filling it with gel of the same consistency as the mesh that she had used previously and was now part of her regular surgical kit. She added a few drops of the mesh and waited for the brain to stabilise. She left the local surgeons to clean up and close the skull. The patient was then taken back to his suite where the family could pray.

Freddie texted Ingrid and reassured her that there was nothing he could add at that stage as she had all she needed, but if there were problems, he could send over some other material. He then brought her up to date with developments in Cairo and the activities of their latest recruit, Carlo.

Ingrid caught the first plane back to Cairo after instructing the local team on how to proceed. When she touched down she found that the new Confederate State of Egypt was already looking much different. As they landed, she was surprised to see that, rather than the oriental backdrop she had experienced before in Cairo, there were neon signs for KFC, McDonald's, Dunkin' Donuts and advertisements for casinos and topless bars. She was spared the formalities of immigration and there was a stretch limo ready to take her to the government department that housed Freddie and his friends. A marine made sure she was taken directly through to Freddie's office. Apart from Freddie, who was now in a sharp suit, were several others similarly dressed, but with facial scars and large gnarled hands and bulging jackets. The conversation was in heavily-accented English with Italian words thrown in.

'You know Carlo but you have not met his friends, Ingrid, they are from all over the USA and also Sicily. I have appointed Carlo as Minister of Culture and you may have seen some of the changes as you came in, as we are building all these places to give work to the local people. We are also bringing in my good friend who is an ex commissioner of the Metropolitan Police at Scotland Yard to run an effective police force and secret service,' announced Freddie.

Ingrid looked at the assembled group of elder statesmen and then looked at Freddie and nodded to him and she gestured for him to come to her office. A large flagon of Chianti was passed round to the members and Havana cigars were either placed in the top pocket or clipped and lit with a jewel-encrusted lighter. Freddie looked a little sheepish, as he was led over to the Ministry of Health.

The Ministry turned out to be a rather grand establishment nearby as Ingrid flashed her card to be led up to a room with a bed that could easily accommodate half a football team. The decor was oriental but there was a well-stocked minibar and a vase that had a red rose replenished on a daily basis. Hotel staff was available around the clock to provide snacks and personal services. Freddie and Ingrid wasted no time in utilising the vast bed after which they helped themselves to the refreshments.

'Freddie, what have you done here? It's like Chicago in the nineteen thirties, run by the mafia but without prohibition,' pointed out Ingrid.

'Ah, but they still don't allow murdering,' said Freddie.

'They will do before long,' said Ingrid with a sigh.

'Well this is not quite the US, it's the CS, the Confederate States, everyone needs a little competition these days,' said Freddie in mitigation.

'And that is good is it?' asked Ingrid.

'Well it hasn't done much harm in the land of the free, which reminds me, we need a national anthem and a constitution and then we will be up there with the best of them and officially the thirteenth state of the CSA,' announced Freddie triumphantly.

'But don't we need a police force and a CIA as well as an organised military?' asked Ingrid.

'All in good time dear, all in good time,' said Freddie.

There was a knock on the door, followed by the words room service, and then a dull thump, and the patter of footsteps down the corridor. Freddie opened the door gingerly and a small plump man covered in food and drink slumped in to the room. On further inspection, he appeared to be dead with a tight ligature of wire around his neck, as a smart man in a striped suit could be seen striding down the corridor as if he was in a hurry. Freddie noticed that the man was not actually plump but had something strapped round his body underneath his bellman's uniform, and there was a pained grin on his blue face. Freddie shrank back looking grey and hurriedly rang the front desk. There was the familiar sound of civil disorder outside and Ingrid parted the curtains and witnessed a small group of freedom fighters with rocket-propelled grenades and machine guns whilst their compadres were firing in the air shouting slogans, with wild eyes and balaclava helmets. At that moment a fleet of saloons slowly drove past as bursts of machine gun fire mowed down the freedom fighters only to do a U-turn and have a re-run to finish off the stragglers. Freddie turned to Ingrid:

'Who was it that poured scorn on the mafia?' asked Freddie with a smirk.

By this time the local militia had responded to Freddie's call and they began to remove the room service whilst the body of the bellman was isolated out of the public area and covered with sand bags. Painstakingly, they cut through Velcro and wires and dumped the improvised bomb that had been strapped to him into a reinforced container, as the man was placed in a body bag labelled food waste. Outside, the emergency services and the Confederate militia checked for any potential threat, firing the occasional round into bodies that moved or cried out. They wore large Stetsons with CSA on the front and pyramid insignia on their arms, but that southern drawl was unmistakeable and Ingrid noticed some rather swarthy types in plainer uniforms performing the more menial tasks.

'By god Freddie, they've even brought back slavery,' said Ingrid with some alarm.

'Well it's not as it looks, these are just the fledgling local native militia, being trained on the job, and anyway, I am bringing in a good mate of mine next week to tidy up the job descriptions,' said Freddie, reassuringly.

'Oh well everything will be OK I'm sure,' said Ingrid sarcastically.

'Don't be like that Ingrid, we're not all chinless imbeciles wasting daddy's money on loose women, booze and snorting,' pointed out Freddie.

'Like you then,' said Ingrid, smiling.

'Oh that's a bit naughty; anyway this chap Bill Stickleback has spent a good part of his life tracking down head-hunting pygmies in the rainforests. What he doesn't know---'

'Yes, yes Freddie, just your type but how will he help us?' asked Ingrid.

'Undercover work, he will head the FBI and he will be answerable to me as Minister of Defence. This sort of thing will become a rarity when we are organised,' replied Freddie.

'It will definitely be a rarity if you manage to murder everyone. What about lawyers, are we sorting that out?' asked Ingrid.

'Oh yes,' reassured Freddie.

'I have to take off my hat to you Freddie,' said Ingrid.

'I didn't notice that you had anything on,' said Freddie.

Ingrid's phone rang; it was the personal assistant of the Drohobyczerrebbe asking to speak with her.

'The rebbe wants me to express his sincere gratitude to you for saving his life and restoring him to the robust health that he has enjoyed in the past. He feels that Elohim has acted through you and he wants me to tell you that if he or his followers can be of help at any time you only need to call, but not on the Sabbath or the high holy days, you understand.'

'Well that is very kind, but I was only doing my job and it was my pleasure,' said Ingrid.

'Well, if this is how you do your job, you must certainly be blessed and may the almighty give you the strength and longevity to help many others in the same way. You know that the rebbe is following closely the changes in your land and he approves wholeheartedly,' said the assistant.

'Many thanks again and shalom,' said Ingrid.

'Shalom.'

'Who was that?' asked Freddie.

'Oh just a grateful patient, you remember another

one we used the mesh on. He's made a full recovery,' said Ingrid.

'And he is?' asked Freddie.

'Oh, just the Drohobyczerrebbe, a sympathiser to the cause apparently,' explained Ingrid.

'Oh yes, I am aware that the ultra-Orthodox Jewish community are really a state within a state in Israel. We are contemplating offering them statehood within the CSA,' said Freddie.

'So you are gathering all the disenfranchised groups under the Confederate banner, Freddie?'

'Well that's the current policy, unless you can figure out a better one?'

There was another call for Ingrid; it was from the personal assistant of one of the Gulf State princes.

'Hello, I am ringing on behalf of his Highness, who wishes to express his gratitude for what you have done for him. He is back to normal now, working like six men but eternally grateful to you, with the Allah's support. He has asked me to say that if there is anything he can do to help, then just say and it will be done, money is no object.'

'That is most generous, but there is no need, I am just pleased to hear that he is progressing so well,' said Ingrid.

'No, the prince insists, and although he knows you are busy helping others, when you are ready, just get in touch and we will arrange it.'

'Many thanks,' said Ingrid.

'And that?' asked Freddie.

'You are so nosy, it is an old flame, no, only joking, that was the prince with the gel, he is doing well also and he has offered us unlimited financial help for whatever we want,' said Ingrid.

Freddie had resigned himself to the fact that he had aligned himself with the closest to a modern saint that

102

was around. He sighed and they left to spend the night somewhere more civilised.

13

When taking off in the hours of darkness it is customary to dim the lights on civil aircraft flights, but the lights were constantly dimmed on the RAF Hercules planes that leave Camp Bastion. The 04.00 departure had as many infantrymen and their kit that could be squeezed on board and, in addition, Diogenes and the failed suicide bomber, who was handcuffed to two military policemen. He was wearing a fixed grin but said nothing apart from giggling from time to time whilst his feet and wrists were connected in a rather neat crossover pattern using heavy chains. Diogenes was the only passenger not in some form of uniform, as even the bomber had a rather garish yellow tracksuit. The soldiers had never met Diogenes before, but news travelled fast on a rather isolated military camp, and Diogenes had attracted a cult status. One of the squaddies was the first to approach the hero.

'That was a mighty fine mission you performed back there, sir,' said the squaddie.

'It was nothing,' remarked Diogenes.

'You mean you do this all the time. It makes our missions look boring compared to your own,' said the awestruck squaddie.

'Well it's not really a mission, I just do work, but I do it on my own, but I need people like you as a backup,' pointed out Diogenes, in mitigation.

'Well we all think you are something very special and we have got together to give you a souvenir of your stay at Bastion.'

Diogenes smiled as he unwrapped an action man soldier with a mobile phone as all the others clapped, only for the sergeant major to tell them all to shut up. The pilot announced that they were en route to RAF

Brize Norton where they would disembark and refuel ready for the next leg of the trip. Most of the soldiers would be going home on leave from there and others would join them. It was a far cry from business class and free-flowing single malt for Diogenes, but he made do with some lager passed round from a crate.

The landing was on time and Diogenes found that the military pilots did not bother with all the niceties of providing trolley dollies, and the most well secured passenger was the suicide bomber. The commanding officer at Brize Norton was most obliging (he must have been radioed ahead) and he immediately agreed to pass on the container with Diogenes's IED samples to Professor Bi in Geneva.

Diogenes was dispatched to the NAFFI and wasted no time in stocking up with single malt and cigarettes, with the Hercules in the aviation fuel department, and before long they were ready to leave with a different, much smaller group of soldiers. The pilot announced that it would be a ten hour trip but there was no hint as to the destination and there was never any mention of refreshments. It was the responsibility of each soldier to stock up in the NAAFI. The suicide bomber was given the food that no-one had chosen. He had declined to say anything, but would push food in his mouth and drink anything available.

Diogenes noticed that the only person on the flight that he recognised was the suicide bomber, and he was showing no sign of becoming more rational. He wondered how long the man would stay like this and after making some calculations on his BlackBerry he came to the conclusion that, as no-one was operating this form of restraint, there could not be an answer, only some vague hypotheses. As he observed the grimacing and tried to understand the babbling he could discern no links, and any attempt to get on the bomber's wavelength was not even acknowledged. The other passengers were a different breed of soldier, they were thickset and appeared to be pumped up with anabolic steroids and were taking in turns to do press-ups and other manoeuvres in the cabin. In contrast, Diogenes appeared puny and, in between slurps from his whisky and sleep, he fiddled with his BlackBerry. Eventually the plane was brought in to land but to Diogenes's dismay there was no runway visible and, from the swaying and rocking, this was a dirt track. Everybody disembarked and the prisoner and Diogenes were left to wait. After some officials had spoken to an accompanying officer, they were allowed off and Diogenes accompanied the prisoner to the base hospital and was introduced to the doctor.

'Bienvenida and welcome to camp Phoenix and thank you for the safe delivery of our friend here, how about we go for a debrief to my office, no,' said the rather swarthy looking doctor who was covered in sweat and grime.

'Thank you, gratias, doctor, this particular gentleman was in the process of killing himself and all the rest of the people in the hospital when I had to intervene,' explained Diogenes.

'Intervene, I see, and what exactly did you have to do?' asked the camp doctor.

'I would love to tell you, but one, it is classified and two, it is a work in progress,' explained Diogenes.

'He doesn't look like he knows anything, is he loco like this all the time?' asked the camp doctor.

'It would seem so, but he will eat and drink,' pointed out Diogenes.

'And is there anything special you want us to do with him?' asked the camp doctor.

'I would just sit on him for a while, but I am not here because of him,' said Diogenes.

'Oh really, so how can we help you?' asked the camp doctor.

'Well, I assume you have some other suicide bombers in here?' asked Diogenes.

'Oh yes, they have their own accommodation, you can take your pick, was there any particular type you wanted?' said the camp doctor.

'Well I need some DNA from them, but that is not the reason I came,' said Diogenes.

'DNA is no problem, but what else is there?' queried the camp doctor.

'This may sound odd, but I need a sample of brain tissue,' announced Diogenes.

'Brain tissue, it is odd, but even more odd is how we can get some for you, they are hardly going to volunteer to donate some,' said the camp doctor.

'Yes, I had thought of that. Is anyone scheduled to have a general anaesthetic soon?' asked Diogenes.

'Let me see, ah yes, number 724 is having wisdom teeth removed tomorrow morning. I suppose we could just say there was an unexpected complication and we had to intervene to preserve life,' the camp doctor suggested.

'I would have thought he would be happier if you killed him,' said Diogenes.

'It is a she actually, and no they all want to live and they are sticklers for the Geneva Convention. Dying is of no value unless you get all the publicity and get on the list of martyrs. Many of these individuals are, how can I put it, lacking in intellectual capacity and were duped into volunteering. Indeed in some parts of Asia suicide bombing is used as part of the system of barter,' explained the camp doctor.

'So that is OK then,' said Diogenes.

'No problem, is there any part of the brain you would like?' asked the camp doctor.

'Ideally I would like a portion of the left temporoparietal region but that is a bit deep, so any bit will do,' said Diogenes.

The next morning Diogenes was guided to a part of the clinical area to wait for his sample and helped himself to a few swigs from his whisky bottle. The staff all wore camouflage uniforms as they went about their medical duties and these were covered in surgical greens in other areas. Diogenes wondered why people liked uniforms so much. He was usually to be seen in some jeans and a jumper and, as he had little time for laundry, he just bought refills whenever he could whilst disposing of the current ones in a bin in the clothes shop. His sample bottle was not long arriving and he was shown to his accommodation in the officers' mess and promised roast for his evening meal.

Diogenes was ready for the early morning turn around flight the next day to the UK with his sample and after another traumatic landing the pilot explained that he was practising evasion of rocket-propelled grenades. A car was supplied and he headed into central London and delivered his sample to the department of nanobiology at the University. Marie had arranged to meet him in the nanobiological liaison laboratory and he noticed that the walls were lined with whiteboards covered with chemical symbols and the centre of the room had glassware and computer-linked analysis equipment. Marie filled Diogenes in with her research progress but she was intrigued to see the refrigerated flask that Diogenes had imported from Bastion. Diogenes suggested that he leave it in her safe keeping whilst they got a bite to eat in the Café Morocco round the corner followed by some single malt and a coffee at hers. Marie was small and slender with brown hair and a cute turned up nose that fitted in with her French origins. She had sexual energy that seemed to escalate with time, but it was blended with a mixture of guile and humour that made her irresistible. After breakfast they reconvened in the laboratory where Diogenes explained that he was looking at receptors in a piece of brain tissue and he would like to leave some of it with her so that she could measure the density of dopamine receptors in it against the receptors in rats with simulated paranoia. He explained that he was looking to her to be his principle research assistant. Marie flushed even though she was aware that he had other collaborators in Geneva, but the day had been by far the best of her life so far and she blew a kiss as Diogenes left and headed off to central London.

Diogenes met Mordechai McIntyre, literary agent, in his customary position in the Nelson's Column.

'Long time no see. Have you forgotten about our book?' asked Mordechai.

'Forgotten, I have just been saving the world,' said Diogenes.

'You know there is something about you that tells me that you are not joking,' said Mordechai.

'Did you get the latest chapters, Mordechai?' asked Diogenes.

'Chapters, what chapters. No I jest, of course I did. Look I don't know about you, but I am getting more confused as we go on. I don't have a clue where we're heading and the mixture of techno-jargon and military gung ho is frightening,' pointed out Mordechai.

'But it's supposed to be, can't you see?' explained Diogenes.

'But the others are not like this.'

'My point exactly, if they were, then I wouldn't be here. Isn't it more exciting like this?'

'Can I just ask you one thing?' said Mordechai.

'Sure fire away,' said Diogenes.

'Do you really think that one day in the foreseeable

future we will be able to manipulate molecules to alter people's brains like this?'

'Oh no, not in the foreseeable future' replied Diogenes.

'Well that is gratifying,' said Mordechai.

'Not in the foreseeable future, we are doing this now,' pointed out Diogenes.

Mordechai looked rather green and his beer suddenly tasted very odd. Diogenes swilled down the remains of his single malt and after glancing at his literary agent, he decided that this was part of his flamboyant persona and needed no special attention. After a wave goodbye, by which time the agent was looking pinker, he picked up some clean clothes at Heathrow airport and caught the first plane to Geneva.

Professor Bi greeted Diogenes at the door with a wide grin. 'We've done it; we have some results, quickly come into the lab, whilst I go through it with you. This is the analysis of the sample from the IEDs you sent over and I also managed to compare it with some explosives from the UN arms dump up the road'.

'And was there a difference?' asked Diogenes.

'Most certainly there was. The IED sample had a tenfold excess of double-bonds compared with the normal. It seems the terrorists are obtaining this exceptionally lethal mixture from somewhere and that is why they are so successful,' explained the professor.

'And how will this help us?' asked Diogenes.

'I thought you would ask that and so let me introduce you to Professor Schweinfurtel, who is an expert in military chemistry and will take over and tell you what he has devised,' said Professor Bi.

'Ah, excuse my English, but in order to reduce the number of double-bonds we need small angle x-rays,' said Professor Schweinfurtel.

'So how does this translate into the combat

situation, professor?' asked Diogenes.

'Ah, like so, we can attach this rod to conventional machine guns or this tube arrangement to military vehicles and this is connected to a small pack powered by the vehicle battery,' explained Schweinfurtel as he manipulated the equipment that he had manufactured.

'And can you say exactly how it works?' asked Diogenes.

'Within a ten metre radius it detonates the device and instead of an explosion you get something like, how do you say, a damp squib,' said Schweinfurtel.

'How long before we can get these manufactured?' asked Diogenes.

'It is a simple and cheap process and so with the will, we can produce them in a few days,' said Schweinfurtel.

'Ah but you mentioned the will, that is a political problem,' said Diogenes.

'My boy, we are in Geneva, these Eurocrats can move fast if we can sell it to them and if it means jobs for people in member states,' explained Professor Schweinfurtel.

Diogenes moved towards the nanobiology labs with his sample, which just involved walking in the direction of the sounds of monkeys and rats squealing.

14

Ingrid checked through her diary which was bulging with extra sheets of paper that she had stapled on when her arrangements changed. Although she was very organised she usually channelled this through her personal assistant whilst she just stuffed another post-it into her diary. Due to the delicacy of the contents, this operation was much like her surgical ones, but she arrived at today's appointments only to find it clear except for an entry which stated travel to Nashville. She turned the page to find that she was booked to sing at a large launch event for the CSA international congress. She found an envelope with a wad of tickets, the first one being a flight from Cairo and her VIP pass. After an overnight rest she made her way to the airport and flew to Nashville.

Ingrid was in the VIP section of the Tennessee Titans football stadium in Nashville. The chairman was one Wilbur La Rochelle, who hailed from Cajun country and could speak French in a manner that made most Frenchmen feel ill. Luckily he stuck to English and the audience consisted of just about every state that ever had Confederate aspersions.

There was South Carolina, Mississippi, Florida, Alabama, Georgia, Louisiana, Texas, Virginia, Arkansas, Tennessee, North Carolina, Kentucky, Missouri, Maryland, Delaware, West Virginia, Oklahoma and Arizona as well as delegations from the Cherokee, Seminole, Chickasaw and Choctaw Indians. There were veterans present as well as serving military but not in their USA fatigues. They wore the grey uniform coats of the 1860s and wore either the kepi or the officers' Stetsons with the toggles lying on the front brim. The music was loud and country and the food was chicken and fries rather than the Yankee burgers and hot dogs. Amongst the delegations was the latest Confederate state of Egypt, the pyramid state, with flag-waving members and an assortment of fez and kafir wearers along with the Stetsons. General La Rochelle addressed the group of around fifty thousand delegates.

'I am proud to welcome y'all to this, the first delegation of the Confederate States of America. You have all heard the expression "The South Will Rise Again", well it has and here we are. It has been over one hundred and fifty years since we last got together and that's way too long. We're not going to let that happen again.

In those days we were known as the slave states and lately, it seems to me that we have been the slaves, not just to the Yankees, but also to the rest of the world and the United Nations. They get us to fight their wars, give them food and look after their sick, and what do we get? You've got it, diddly-squat. Well each and every one of you has played your part in this historic occasion and this is only the beginning. I would especially like to welcome our first delegates from the Asian continent and I know that they will not be the last, can you stand up please and let everyone see you.

But nothing must deter us from our own country-style celebrations and we have Sue Dakota as well as T-Bone Redneck and his Galveston Rebels as well as a top grade Cajun band from my own backyard. So welcome and bienvenue to the Confederate freedom celebrations and let's enjoy the music and food.'

As the arena vibrated to the music, Sue's BlackBerry was vibrating with a text from Saudi Arabia telling her that a private jet was at her disposal to take her to a meeting with a royal delegation as soon as she had a window.

After a restless night and jet lag she managed to get to the airport to find that she was the only passenger on the Lear Jet from Nashville International Airport and then onto Chicago and Jeddah, before the royal limo whisked her off to a hotel in preparation for the visit. The meeting with her royal hosts was in a vast palace with handwoven rugs and relics from wild animal hunts adorning the walls. The royal prince was very much in control and he rose to meet Ingrid as she entered in a smart business suit.

'It is a great honour for me to meet you in the flesh. My family never even envisaged that this would be possible in their wildest dreams, but by the grace of Allah and your good self, the impossible has become possible,' said the royal prince in welcoming her.

'It is my pleasure your highness, it is great to see you in such robust health. What can I do for you?' asked Ingrid.

'It is the other way round; it is what we can do for you,' said the prince smiling benignly.

'I see, is there anything you have in mind?' asked Ingrid.

'Well yes, we have been very impressed with your work in neighbouring Egypt and as current chairman of the Arab League, I feel that others could gain from your good work. I am aware that all of this needs funding and so I am giving you an open chequebook to continue with this,' announced the prince.

'Is there any particular project that you have in mind?' asked Ingrid.

'Yes, it is Syria at the moment. We can't just allow this chaos to continue, it is bad for our international standing. I have arranged for you to meet the Minister of Health for Syria with our own minister in Damascus for some preliminary discussions, all the logistics will be taken care of, meanwhile if you just avail yourself of our hospitality we will set things up,' said the prince.

Ingrid contacted Freddie on his new intercontinental hot line in his position as Secretary of State for Asia in the Confederate government.

'I may have some business for you, Freddie.'

'Don't you think we have enough here, Ingrid?' said Freddie.

'Why what is happening?' asked Ingrid.

'Well, we have a turf war going on with Carlo taking on Bill Stickleback. It's the Mafia versus the Feds all over again,' said Freddie, in an agitated state.

'That doesn't sound like you. What do you mean, what's happening on the ground?' asked Ingrid.

'On the ground, there are bombings, drive-by shootings, assassinations and G men all over, with informers and large numbers of dollars being passed around,' said Freddie in desperation.

'And the rest of the population?' asked Ingrid.

'Well, they just sit in the cafes on their hookahs and barter in the bazaars as before, oblivious to the chaos,' said Freddie.

'You mean they are not affected?' asked Ingrid.

'It isn't that they are not affected, they are used to this, it is just the fact that it is foreigners that are doing it to them this time,' pointed out Freddie.

'So what is the solution?' asked Ingrid.

'No solution my dear, I am sure that it will all work its way through the system, in time, like the nineteen thirties. So what have you got for me?' asked Freddie.

'I'm not sure, but I will let you know after I have returned from the road to Damascus,' said Ingrid.

'Very biblical Ingrid, I didn't know you were religious,' said Freddie.

'I'm not, but wait and see and just try to twist a few arms so that we are in overall control before it all falls apart,' said Ingrid.

Ingrid had accompanied the Saudi minister on his plane to Damascus and after landing there was a short drive to the presidential palace. The roads were lined with army and police personnel as well as artillery. Ingrid noticed that the roads had large potholes and many of the buildings were stained black and were adorned with shell holes or masonry falling down. Small arms fire and the odd explosion could be heard in the background and she noticed that her car was not just a top of the range model but it also had blacked out windows and heavy reinforced doors. The journey was silent as nobody spoke and nothing other than the sounds of war could be heard. Three Syrian Ministers of Health were sitting in the meeting room in the presidential palace surrounded by a large array of fruit. Outside the room was a detachment of armed secret service agents with earpieces. The first Syrian Minister of Health was very old and grey and immaculately turned out with half-moon spectacles and a thick dossier of political papers by his side. In contrast, the others at the meeting just had a notepad and mobile phones, whilst Ingrid was just there in person and her Saudi colleague was carrying the papers. Ingrid's medical observation skills noticed that the Syrian's face was a pale green and there was a cold unhealthy sweat on his brow and his hands were shaking. In another place she would have diagnosed heart failure, but an alternative diagnosis was just fear. As they began to slice their fruit some flunkies served drinks with some biscuits.

'I think we had better begin the agenda with the state of the health services here along with the problems that your government are facing,' said the Saudi minister.

'We have no problems here, I have the minutes of all our council meetings which goes to show ----------'

began the Syrian health minister.

'Yes I know all that, but the Arab Association along with the rest of the world have grave doubts about your ability to cope without outside help, and this is why I have brought the new health minister for Egypt to see if she can assist,' pointed out the Saudi.

'I don't know where you get your information from, but Syria is the most stable and oldest democracy in the world and we do not need the help of outsiders, thank you very much,' said the Syrian.

Ingrid was peeling some fruit as the two adversaries were locked head to head in an impasse that was much the same as would have happened in biblical days. The Syrian's voice became more strained as he sought in vain to persuade the Saudi that Syria led the way until a faint gurgle heralded a flushing, as the Syrian slumped with his head banging on the desk on the way to the floor. The flunkies drew their weapons in defence of the realm in fear of an imaginary assailant who might strike again. By this time the Syrian was even more grey with his greenish tinge and Ingrid had pulled him onto the table, scattering the food and drink. After leaving the others to summon for help, Ingrid had commandeered a fruit knife and was deep into the ministerial chest massaging his heart before local medical help had time to arrive. The first ones on the scene were the militia whose instinct was to drag Ingrid off and have her shot for insurrection. She reminded them that she had diplomatic immunity whilst leaving the others to explain what she was doing. By this time the building was surrounded by army units and tanks which the regime had found easier than an ambulance with medics. As the medical emergency continued, the Saudi minister had summoned some high-ranking officials and he made it clear that there had to be change or else they would find that they stood alone, and even their traditional allies like China and Russia may not feel able to support them.

As the Syrian team had arrived with equipment the Syrian minister became stabilised enough to be transported to the presidential hospital within the palace grounds.

Ingrid was on the phone to T-Bone: 'I think we are going to have to move on Syria.'

'How'd you mean move?' asked T-Bone.

'A bit like the Egyptian scenario but this time the natives could be seen as hostile,' explained Ingrid.

'That shouldn't be a problem, do you want me to get the general to mobilise the air force bombers?' asked T-Bone.

'First, I would suggest that I talk to Freddie to see what he can do,' said Ingrid.

It was obvious that their mission in Damascus was not going to progress and Ingrid looked at the chaos and began to panic and she rapidly headed for the airport and the first flight to Cairo.

Back in Egypt Freddie was in his own building organising and co-ordinating the warring factions at the same time as being the vice-chancellor of the university and trying to build it into a world recognised nanabioelectronic centre, when Ingrid entered, with a worried look. Egypt was, if anything, descending more into chaos, and, walking the streets, it was difficult to know which section would haul you off into a back alleyway. Bill Stickleback entered with a pin-striped suit and a guard's tie. He had to bend to get through the doorway, he was shaven headed with hands that could be used in a pizza oven and he gave the impression that there was little he had not turned his hand to. After the usual introductions they retired to a corner of Freddie's vast office.

'Listen chaps, we need to mount a task force to take

over Syria,' said Freddie.

'Take over Syria, just like that, don't you think we have enough here?' asked Bill.

'I don't think it will take much, they seem to be on their knees, and they are there for the taking,' said Freddie.

'I could cobble together a snatch force in a week or two if you like,' said Bill.

'It's going to take more than that, Bill. We need some air power, a no-fly zone and as the USA is reluctant, this is a chance for the CSA to take over,' said Ingrid.

'And we need to have someone on the inside who we can trust,' said Freddie.

'I know a good chap in Syria, he's the main man in the Damascus Hebrews and he has no truck with the current regime,' said Bill.

Ingrid's BlackBerry rang; it was the chief envoy of the Drohobyczerrebbe.

'The rebbe is asking after you and as he is now in robust health, he is anxious to help you in any way possible,' said the envoy.

'It's great to hear that, give him my regards. There is one thing he can do. Does he know anyone in Syria who can be relied on?' asked Ingrid.

'Actually he does, indeed he was only talking to him this afternoon. A gentleman by the name of Tamuz Halevy,' said the envoy.

15

Diogenes had spent most of his working life in large laboratory blocks with their never-ending corridors of rooms and removable name tags in metal holders on the doors. Sometimes there were up to four professors in one room. Most of the professors designated to the room did not use it.

He was used to the security checks before he was allowed to enter the animal laboratories deep in the bowels of the building and happily made up answers that he thought the uniformed robotic guards wanted to hear. As he entered, he could hear the squeals and barking and he could smell the antiseptic sawdust that was sprinkled on the floor of the cages. A helpful assistant pointed out Professor Bi who was lying prone under a large machine with wires and glass spheres emanating from all angles. As he entered the mega-lab, he noticed the professor who was working with a soldering iron and a variety of long metal implements underneath an entangled mesh of coloured wires. Diogenes tried to attract his attention but he noticed that the professor was wearing ear protectors and so he gently touched his leg. The professor arched his back as a reflex to this unexpected incursion and his head came into contact with part of the machine, producing a trickle of blood and a long Chinese curse.

'Who is this in my laboratory?' shouted the Chinaman when he had come round enough to speak English.

'Don't worry sir; it is only me with some interesting material for you,' announced Diogenes.

The professor extracted himself from the machine and pointed to a dust-covered cupboard with a red cross on it. Diogenes sprang into action and sifted through the yellowing packets of bandages, antiseptics and cotton wool and noticed that they were well past their expiry date.

'Don't you have regular checks on these boxes?' mumbled Diogenes as he fished out some gauze.

'The organization is on an economy drive and we have to get at least five signatures before we can spend any money at all,' said the professor, as he stemmed the bleeding with wipes used for animal hygiene.

'Just let me help,' said Diogenes.

'Haven't you done enough damage so far?' asked the patient.

'Look, let's just take a hands-on approach and patch you up, instead of launching a research project, otherwise nothing will happen'.

Diogenes skilfully applied the contents of the box to the wound with a bandage, as he had done many times as a front line medic in the army. The professor relaxed and even managed to smile and inquired after what had brought Diogenes to visit again.

'I don't know whether you remember but I was concerned with the continuing problem of suicide bombers and I have been working on a way to counter this problem. I have managed to get a sample from the brain of a failed bomber and my idea is for us to analyse this with a view to finding how they differ from the norm,' explained Diogenes.

'How did you -------?' asked the professor.

'Don't ask, but this is hopefully the temporoparietal region and we need to compare this with other samples, either from primates, or from patients who are having neurosurgical procedures, or maybe some transplant donors who have intact temporoparietal regions,' said Diogenes.

'And you think we can do this?' asked the professor.

'I think if anyone can, you can,' said Diogenes with

some confidence.

'It might need funding,' pointed out the professor.

'I can sort that out, as most of the world's wealthiest nations are at threat and would write open cheques for this project. It's of the utmost priority and we need to be able to translate the findings electronically, so that we can alter these impulses in live brains and stop the bombers in their tracks,' explained Diogenes.

'You ask a lot and I don't have the skills to change brain impulses by electronic manipulation, but I might know someone who can'.

'I am depending on you,' said Diogenes as he attempted to find his way out.

After getting lost a few times and being wrongly directed by assistants, who seemed to speak every language but his own, Diogenes was outside the building and headed for the Café Morocco. After a large whisky he began to relax and as he was about to order some pastries, he received a short text. His controllers in London had arranged for him to attend a meeting in the Knesset in Israel with prominent Israeli politicians the next day, and prior to this there was a room reserved near to Geneva airport. He forgot about the pastry and before long he was in his room drinking his usual superior blend of single malt. The room service contained enough stodge to make sure that he didn't suffer stomach pangs, which were not unusual when he forgot to eat.

He was at the airport early and passed through customs rapidly and after yet more single malt he was getting to the point where he was nearing incoherence. On arrival in Tel Aviv he had to be x-rayed and hand searched and he found that his diplomatic status was ignored. When he showed them his credentials he was politely informed that just about every terrorist in their jails came into the country with CD status. He pointed out that it had been the Knesset that had asked him to enter their country, and after some phone calls he was eating Mediterranean food and fruit in a modern office in the parliament building. Due to the rather public nature of the meeting, the topics had to be vague as national security and settlements were high on the agenda of all their meetings. Diogenes was looking bored and the chairman suggested that he have a one to one with a major general down the corridor to deal with his specific issues. He was led, with a plate of water melon, to a smaller office where a large man with a uniform covered in medal ribbons, and one eye, rose to meet him. As he got closer he could see that the major general was in a wheelchair and had scarring on his face. The major general pointed to a chair and pressed a button to summon yet more refreshments.

'Welcome to Israel and the nerve centre of the IDF operations. We are hoping you can help us with what has become a real problem,' announced the officer with an American accent.

'I hope I can be of some use,' pointed out Diogenes.

'I am sure you can. As you know, we have been profoundly affected by suicide bombers along with many others in this region. We are not known for our altruism in Israel, but in this case we have mutual interests with much of the world and we are interested in trying to neutralize this, if there is a way'.

'Yes I am aware of this, and I am doing what I can and I am quite optimistic that we can come up with something,' explained Diogenes.

'There is another problem, which has not been mentioned. At present we are not enjoying much support internationally and even the USA and much of the West, our traditional allies, are hostile and pro-Palestinian'.

'Why is that?' asked Diogenes.

'We are seen as a military threat to the area, and our indigenous population, the Israelis are seen as arrogant and people have forgotten about the Holocaust, and the whole Palestinian and Arab identity has become fashionable.'

'But there was a time when the Palestinians were hated after the Black September and the PLO atrocities,' said Diogenes.

'That is only remembered by older people and the Arabs have successfully played the race card and, as they are many in number and widespread, they are able to shout louder,' explained the soldier.

'What did you have in mind?' asked Diogenes.

'It's not for me to say, but some people think that you are the only one could help with this.'

'Do you have a neurobiologist in the building who can help me?' asked Diogenes.

'Actually to look at me you would not think that I was a researcher in this field before I was drafted in to lead patrols near the border areas, but I still have an intact brain, so I will try to help,' said the soldier.

'Before I go let me explain where we are so far. We are looking at abnormal salience. This is how people perceive things. So most people see, for example, a large metal structure with seats, an engine, a windscreen, doors that makes a noise and moves along. They would call it a car or a vehicle. Others may look at the same object and not be able to connect these features in the same way. So they may misidentify this and so they may feel threatened by it. That could lead to anger, confusion or even violence,' explained Diogenes.

'So how does this move us forward, sir?' asked the soldier.

'That's the difficult bit; this abnormal salience is channelled through nerve fibres and receptors in the brain to the temporal lobe. So if we can alter these pathways, then we can change salience from abnormal to normal and vice versa'.

'Can you translate that into practical applied science?' asked the soldier.

'Not yet, but if we can make people mad, and if these people are high-level Palestinian representatives, then this can be in your favour'.

'But they are not going to volunteer to undergo some experimental procedure,' pointed out the general.

'Ah that is the challenge. We have to make a system where they don't know what is happening, i.e. it is covert, so it is simply the delivery of the process that we need to perfect.'

The major general looked stunned as he typed Diogenes's words on to his laptop and perspired at the thought of it. Diogenes finished off the fruit and looked at all the trophies and certificates around the office.

'Major general, do you have any Mossad in here?' asked Diogenes, not realizing the complexity of the question.

'Well, I can't answer that, but I will ring down and if you go to room thirteen after this, they may be able to help. I must say this is brilliant, just brilliant,' said the soldier, in awe.

Diogenes smiled as he was escorted to room thirteen. His escort wore military fatigues and was used to long marches in full kit and was moving at a brisk pace and Diogenes struggled keeping up, hampered by his alcohol consumption. When they did arrive Diogenes was struggling to breathe due to his asthma. There was nothing on the door except for a hole and the door opened as he approached. It had one chair and a notice in several languages that beckoned him to wait. After five minutes another door opened and a green sign ordered him to enter. In the next room a screen with a robot head asked him why he was here. He explained about being invited and having met the major general and then he was ushered in by a slim swarthy man in a black polo neck and matching trousers who beckoned him to sit down opposite an officer at a desk which was covered with papers and gadgets and he noticed that there were CCTV screens all over the walls.

'What can we do for you?' asked the officer.

'I thought it was the other way round, you invited me,' answered Diogenes.

'We don't have the need for time-wasters, we are a professional organization with a large responsibility for the security of the country and we are doing very nicely without anyone's help,' pointed out the agent.

'Well if you are convinced of this, that is fine but I am a busy scientist who has other things to do and so I would recommend that you step back a little and listen to me. Anyway, the way I see it, you are not doing nicely at all, in fact you are leading this country to the brink of destruction and you need me more than I need you,' said Diogenes, who was getting impatient.

'You have some cheek; I could make you disappear within minutes,' explained the officer.

'I am sure you can, but can you not see that by doing that, you make yourselves a laughing stock in the eyes of the rest of the world, and anyway, I can do all that quicker, more efficiently and cheaper than yourselves,' said Diogenes.

'OK, OK I will listen, but only because I have been ordered to, so make it snappy,' said the agent.

'I think the main problem is whether you have the wit to understand what I am about to say. Anyway, because of this arrogance, and other factors, the world is trying its hardest not to hate you at the moment,' said Diogenes.

'What do we care?'

'Well if you want to be abandoned and stand alone against the world, then that would make sense'.

'We have done this before through our short history and before that the holocaust and the pogroms in Eastern Europe and we are still here.'

'Still here, just about, the way you are going there will be a nuclear war and none of us will be here. Why don't you just think about how you got to this?' asked an increasingly frustrated Diogenes who was wondering why he had bothered to come at all.

'It is not our fault, we are just persecuted,' trotted out the agent, as if from a manual.

'No-one wants to persecute you, can you not see that you are part of the problem, anyway I am here to work on the mindset of Palestinians to try to make them less effective'.

'You can't change them, it is fixed,' explained the agent.

'A bit like you then; in fact, I think I can change them, although listening to you I am not sure it will change anything.'

'Only we can do this and we don't need the help of an outsider, thank you,' pointed out the officer nearing the end of his patience.

'Are you sure you want me to leave with that message?' asked Diogenes.

'Why not, what are you going to do? Why should I care?' said the agent.

'Can you get someone to take me to your Minister of Defence?' asked Diogenes sensing that he was not going to get any further.

'Minister of Defence, what do you want with him?'

'As you just said, why should you care, just get me out of here.'

He was tipped out into the corridor and found the

military escort waiting for him. He was taken to the office of the minister, up various elevators and down concrete corridors, as sweat poured off him.

The minister was talking to the prime minister as Diogenes was welcomed in and offered a well-upholstered armchair in the finest leather.

'How did you get on in room thirteen?' asked the minister.

16

Ingrid was drinking Turkish coffee in the Café Morocco in a small square in Damascus. Her Saudi friend was commiserating about their lack of progress at the meeting and the poor state of health of the Syrian minister. The café was crammed with locals who were shuffling their worry beads. The proprietor had several coffee pots on the go in between his hookah and a cheroot. The business in good luck charms and amulets was brisk, in defiance of the world recession. The Saudi minister opened the conversation:

'I am not sure where we go from here.'

'There is always hope and I think the state of health of the Syrian health minister proves that the government are more desperate than us,' said Ingrid.

'How do you mean?' asked the Saudi minister.

'I think they have run out of credible solutions and there is only so long that you can survive as a nation without allies.'

'But there are always allies, if not the West or the Arabs there is China or Russia,' pointed out the Saudi minister.

'The traditional allies like the Eastern countries strive for respectability these days and so we are left with countries like Cuba, Venezuela and North Korea.'

'So what is the problem with them?' asked the Saudi minister.

'They are poor and with few resources and they are disorganised, so in reality my people are their only chance as the West has little appetite for intervention after Afghanistan and Iraq,' said Ingrid.

An elderly Arab in ragged clothes and with a limp entered from the street seeking shelter from the war zone. He gestured to the proprietor for a coffee and pulled up a chair at their table.

'Let me introduce myself.'

'Don't tell me, you are Tamuz Halevy,' said Ingrid.

The eyebrows of the Saudi rose as he recognised Tamuz's tribal origins. Tamuz explained:

'I have been asked if I can help here. You are in a difficult situation with an intransigent country that does not know what is best for itself. I am the leader and one of the small numbers of Syrian Hebrews who did not leave all those centuries ago and so we are survivors and if you need anyone to get you out of difficult situations then I am the man.'

'But who are you Tamuz in real terms?' inquired the Saudi minister.

'I can get you access to people who matter and when you meet them you will see that they can make things change,' explained Tamuz.

'But why would you do this?' asked the Saudi minister.

'Quite simply, it is to help with the restoration of the Hebrews to Syria as in biblical times,' answered Halevy.

Ingrid's BlackBerry rang: it was the hospital where they had the Minister of Health. The head doctor spoke to her:

'Your patient is in a poor way. We are all grateful for what you were able to do, but he is not yet clinically stable and any further help would be appreciated. He has heart and brain damage and it is feared that without active intervention he will not be with us much longer.'

'OK, but I need a colleague to fly out from Egypt before we can get to work on this and he will need a lab to work in when he arrives,' explained Ingrid.

'I will arrange a private jet ASAP,' replied the doctor.

The Saudi minister and Tamuz were deep in

conversation about the problem of Syria.

'They are going to have to change or there is no future here,' said the Saudi.

'I am ready to do all I can, as it is my birth right,' said Tamuz.

'It is not just a question of money; it is entrenched attitudes, especially at the top,' said the Saudi.

'We have to create a situation where the leaders are forced to work with us,' said Tamuz.

'How can you do that?' asked the Saudi.

'I've done it before and it rarely fails and I don't need any money.'

'You don't need money?'

'Jews have, for centuries, been brought into countries that have been short of money, all over the world. So they can supply it and I will spend it as a form of investment.'

'But investments can crash in the current climate.'

'Not this one,' announced Tamuz with some confidence.

Freddie had just jetted in and was surveying the scans whilst the Syrian Minister of Health was hanging on to life with tubes emanating from all orifices. It was certainly true to say that his heart was damaged and from the continuous scanning device the heart was more like a small leather bag that twitched a little. His blood was being pumped round his body by one of the state of the art machines with Russian writing and a few Arabic labels. His brain activity was more difficult to estimate but the PET scans together with the MRI scans showed tracts of brain fibres with various levels of disintegration. Whereas some surgeons could have tried a heart transplant, brain damage was not currently treatable. Freddie had set up his mobile laboratory in the biochemistry department and he had imported a mixture of stem cells for the task ahead. The Syrian team had supplied samples from the minister's tissues and Freddie had commandeered all the microscopes whilst he personalised the transplant material.

The operation took about eight hours with teams of assistants from the local services backing up Ingrid and Freddie. After working furiously on the heart and the brain they left the local teams to close up. The next port of call was the Defence office where Tamuz and the Saudi envoy were waiting. Tamuz spoke to vice admiral al-Aleppo, the minister and ex-head of the armed forces.

'We are all most grateful for the assistance with my good friend in Health. What can we do to help?' asked the vice admiral.

'I am here as a Syrian whose family dates back many centuries. We are still loyal to our country and recognise that a strong Syria means a strong Syrian Jewish community,' explained Tamuz.

'So how can you all help?' asked the vice admiral.

'You need an infrastructure and I don't know whether you have kept up with developments in Egypt, but we could do the same for you,' said Ingrid.

'Are you asking us to become a satellite of the West?' asked al-Aleppo.

'No, not at all. We are just talking sponsorship with all the advantages that go with it,' explained the envoy.

'But why should we agree to that?'

'I will hand you over to the Egyptian Minister of Defence,' said the Saudi minister.

'Hello admiral, it is nice to be here but I can't help noticing that the conditions out and about are similar to those that we found when we arrived in Egypt,' said Freddie.

'What do you mean, Syria is the most democratic country on earth. All the citizens love their government and their dear leader and there is hardly any dissent or crime.'

'Can I introduce myself, I am the Saudi health minister but I have a cabinet seat in the new alliance and I am aware of the arrangements within our neighbours. We are not democratic and as a result the presence of dissent or crime is unknown. We are all aware of this but we are not proud of it.'

'So how does this affect the Syrian situation?' asked al-Aleppo.

'Surely you can see what the rest of the world can see, in that you are vulnerable and an invasion is imminent and you may be seen as war criminals,' explained the Saudi.

'So what can you do for us and how much is it going to cost?' asked the Syrian minister.

Tamuz was shaking his head as his colleagues tried to find a way out of this quandary. Either the admiral was someone who had been promoted way above his level of competence or he had been brainwashed like the rest of them, or both. There was a knock on the door by another military man with medals hanging in such profusion that they jangled about as if they were part of an orchestra. He whispered in the admiral's ear, who nodded and winced as he eyed Tamuz with increasing despair. The admiral was trying to smile as the officer left and they resolved the meeting.

'The cabinet has asked me to thank both of you for the miracles you have valiantly performed on my colleague. You will be pleased to know that he is now mobile and asking for his government dispatch boxes,' announced the admiral.

'Well that is good news,' said Ingrid.

'And there is something else,' added the admiral.

'Yes.'

'They have instructed me to go along with your plans for restructuring the country,' said Freddie. 'Do you want me to outline these for you?'

'No, no, that will not be necessary, I will take my leave and send in the civil servants, but meanwhile I will supply you with refreshments,' said al-Aleppo.

Tamuz commandeered the whiteboard and the pens and began by entering the title: "Confederate States of America" and then "Syria, the fourteenth state, the civilisation state". He wrote quickly in bullet points.

-Hookah pipes sponsored by Comanche products Alabama.

-Fast food, kebab burgers and camel burgers with couscous.

-Camel racing sponsored by Palomino from Texas.

-Baby-ware, prams, cots, diapers supplied by the Cradle of Civilisation from the Chickasaw tribes of Oklahoma.

The Syrian symbol will be one of their traditional boats with a red crescent and we will twin the country with Arizona where there is a big Syrian community. Then we supply the infra-structure in the form of the Arizona Militia who are true patriots and link in with the Middle-Eastern Confederate forces.

A civil servant burst in with his notebook as Tamuz wiped off the whiteboard ready for the briefing as the other two managed a smile.

'OK, can you just fill me in with what has been agreed, so that I can set about the implementation?' asked the bureaucrat.

Tamuz took over the conversation after some nods from the rest of the team.

'Rather than going through the details, I will send a colleague of mine in a few days with the final blueprint and then if you get someone to sign it off, we will be ready to go.'

'Can we trust you to act in our interest?' asked the bureaucrat.

'Well your cabinet has approached us to arrange this and when we have the details we do not want to delay, in case scenarios take a different turn and the place becomes a state of emergency and a tinder pot for the whole region,' said Tamuz.

'I don't think the cabinet would take very kindly to being threatened like this,' pointed out the civil servant in a threatening manner.

'Well, it's your decision, but I can tell you, if you end up in a civil war with insurgents taking over, then there will be no hope and it will be too late.'

'Still I like to check up on these matter, so if you excuse me for a few minutes,' said the civil servant.

The team helped themselves to the refreshments as Ingrid received an email. It was headed The University of Iceland, Department of Old Norse. It read, "My dearest daughter Ingrid, long time no see. Reading through all these runes tends to cut you off from the rest of the world. I hear on the grapevine that you are now a diplomat and a government minister. Nothing surprises me about you and I hope they can keep up with you. I am writing to tell you that your mum Anya is now seriously ill in Copenhagen. We are all trying to fix it to get there as soon as we can. Your brother Inge is working at the United Nations for Sweden but is hoping to get there as quickly as he can. At the moment mum is holding her own in the hospital but she is compos mentis and would love the chance to see us all. Love pappi."

The door opened and another civil servant entered.

'I have been sent to tell you that all is OK. If you send your colleague to see me, I am Mahmood al-Aleppo, what is his name?'

'It is Mamser Ha-erev,' said Tamuz.

The sound of a single gunshot could be heard from the lower floors.

17

Diogenes just smiled as he recounted the rather tortuous conversation in room thirteen and it was obvious that the minister had heard all of this before. Although his research was of the utmost significance, particularly in Israel, but also globally, Diogenes found it quite incredible that most of the Israeli hierarchy were so casual. Maybe that was the problem, but certainly it had been allowed to escalate because no-one had taken it seriously enough. Diogenes's phone rang; it was Professor Bi who sounded like his laboratory had gone into overdrive.

'Hello, this is Bi here; I think we may have some information for you. We didn't find a lot in the temporoparietal region of the brain but some of the fibres were quite enlarged and these have been identified as emanating from the orbitofrontal region.'

'That is interesting because we already know that with paranoid patients there are the same brain changes and I didn't think to link paranoia and brainwashing,' said Diogenes.

'There must be some overlap but the question is which of the two conditions is more severe. It's maybe that the paranoia is chronic, and brainwashing is more acute,' said Bi.

'Yes, but the main question is how we can affect rapid changes in these conditions,' pointed out Diogenes.

'I suppose the easy answer is to try some medication,' suggested Bi.

'Yes, but a suicide bomber cannot be medicated and it is not rapid enough. It needs to be instantaneous,' said Diogenes.

'That will be a challenge,' said Bi.

'I'm thinking of electronic modification of the abnormality,' suggested Diogenes.

'You are thinking well out of any box,' said Bi, as he smiled.

The Israeli minister had been listening to this conversation in some awe as he played with his executive toys. Diogenes made a few calculations on his BlackBerry and drank his coffee.

'I don't suppose you have single malt here do you?' he added.

'Single malt, we have Jaffa orange liquor. I can highly recommend it, and it certainly packs a punch,' offered the minister.

'Do Mossad drink this?' asked Diogenes in a humorous aside.

The minister smiled and demonstrated, for the first time in Israel, a sense of humour. Diogenes looked up at the minister and smiled.

'I couldn't trouble you with a request, could I?'

'Try me,' offered the minister.

'What I would like, is to go into one of your asylums and talk to one of your best neuropsychiatrists about checking out some of our theories on some of the patients.'

'Would you like any facilities for this?' asked the minister.

'Well, a laboratory and some advanced scanning equipment would be good if you don't mind.'

'For you, anything, just give me ten minutes, you can see Dr Schloff,' said the minister.

Diogenes entered the University mental hospital with some trepidation, but by the time he had walked about one kilometre down the main drive and passed large numbers of men and women who did not even appear to acknowledge his existence, he had relaxed completely. The gardens were tendered as if someone had measured each leaf and blade of grass with a microtome and this contrasted with the patients, who were dishevelled and bizarre. Some grinned inanely, others talked to themselves, but most of them were just bland. Occasionally patients would converse, even argue, and Diogenes was asked whether he was a doctor by others. At the end of the drive was a large administration block with a sign in Hebrew, Arabic and English instructing visitors to report there. Dr Schloff was seated behind a desk piled high with notes, behind a haze of cigarette smoke.

'How can I help you, sir?' asked the doctor.

'Well I don't know whether you have been briefed, but I have a device that needs to be tested on some of your patients,' announced Diogenes.

'How many do you need?' asked the doctor with minimal interest.

'I thought of three groups of perhaps ten. I need to have ten paranoids, ten schizophrenics and ten normal.'

'I will have no problem with the first two groups but the normals; I can foresee some difficulties there.'

'Do you mean that normal people would not be in here?'

'Oh on the contrary, I am sure there are plenty of those, but we don't know which are which,' said the doctor.

'What about the staff?'

'You think they are normal?' smiled the doctor.

'I see, but I think we will use them anyway, and it is important that they are all randomly mixed with code numbers on them. I will not need to speak to them but if they can all be in a room and I will call them in one by one.'

'When do you want to start?' asked the doctor.

'Is now OK?' asked Diogenes.

Dr Schloff sent for the chief male nurse, an

enormous sleepy looking chap with weeping eczema and a scruffy white coat. He was a man of few words and even fewer enormous steps, as Diogenes had to make sure he didn't lag behind and lose him. Fortunately the nurse's regulation steel toecap boots made a squeak, and his body odour made him easy to detect. Diogenes found out later that he was called the punchbag due to his rather unusual method of calming down the most agitated of inmates. Diogenes was supplied with a room, a chair and a desk with some paper. The patients filed in one after the other with numbers stuck on their foreheads whilst Diogenes operated his BlackBerry. It soon became clear that the highest readings were from the paranoids, followed by the schizophrenics, with the normals last. There were a few outliers, particularly in the staff group, and Diogenes wondered whether he should report this to someone. He came to the conclusion that this would breach confidentiality and probably would make no difference anyway, so he took his leave, being careful not to look too suspicious to avoid being detained.

The question arose as to where suicide bombers would figure on this scale. Were they beyond the paranoids or somewhere between the schizophrenics and the paranoids or were they normal? Diogenes needed to leave Israel.

After disembarking at Heathrow he quickly identified Leonardo and they found a café. Diogenes explained his need for suicide bombers.

'What about the ones you met in Central America?' suggested Leonardo.

'I think they have been contaminated by the system and so from my point of view they are not fresh enough and probably would be invalid for my work. I need some who are about to set out on a mission,' said Diogenes.

'Have you tried to get some in Israel?' asked Leonardo.

'I have just come from there, I think they have done as much as they can, or perhaps I should say, as much as they want to do.'

'You would think it would be in their interest to co-operate with this,' said Leonardo.

'That's what I thought but they have a wholly different agenda from everyone else.'

'So how can we help?' asked Leonardo.

'I am going to have to go to the Afghan-Pakistan border for a while, there is no other way,' pointed out Diogenes.

Diogenes calculated that his best route would be via Lahore where there still was enough British influence to act as a base camp for his manoeuvres. His first class flight passed without incident and an embassy car ferried him direct to the ambassador's PA. Leonardo had a contact in the British embassy. Horatio Pennyfarthing was just under seven feet and wearing the best that Savile Row could supply. Indeed they had to send an agent from Delhi to measure him, and his size sixteen shoes had to be imported. He directed Diogenes to a large cardboard box full of rags and assorted plimsolls.

'Here is your outfit. One set will do, most of the locals manage with that. I have put together some food and papers for you and there are directions to a place where you can stay and a few names of locals who we can trust. I assume you speak the various dialects, so if I were you I would take a quick swig of this, and be on your way on the next train to the border areas. If you can memorise this number, we can get you out ASAP,' explained the giant Horatio.

Diogenes settled in to an apartment overlooking a narrow street crammed with people and the longer he watched the more it appeared that the same faces were reappearing at regular intervals. He reckoned that this meant either they were going in a large circle, or they all looked the same, either due to inbreeding or all having clothes from the same sort of box that Horatio kept in his room. Diogenes had straw bed on a stone floor covered with sawdust that could double as a latrine. There was a tap on the wall and the window looked as if it had once contained glass. He was lucky in some ways, as it appeared from the noise that the other apartments were crammed full of locals. He stumbled down the steps in semi-darkness noting where the concrete had crumbled, and it appeared that a fractured bone in that environment could mean certain death. Once in the street he joined the flowing crowd on their meandering past the stalls selling goods that would be used as landfill in the affluent West. Diogenes was already seeing part of the reason why it was not difficult to recruit suicide bombers. He found some seats and tables set back from the hordes so as to regain some control over his destiny; there was a splintering sign labelled Café Morocco. The waiter did not appear to have washed for some time, but if he had similar accommodation to Diogenes, it was wholly understandable. Hot tea appeared with some pastries on cracked plates and at the same time a collection of beggars, sensing some opportunity, gathered with palms upturned. Diogenes tossed a coin to one but was disappointed that his disguise had little effect and he still stood out as a relatively affluent stranger. The beggars were talking rapidly and noise was escalating like an aeroplane just before take-off. A cleaner old man with a full beard grabbed hold of the biggest beggars and muttered something that Diogenes could not catch, and they ran as a tide of people. The man spoke in Urdu and introduced himself.

'Hello, I am Mohammed Khalil, and I am pleased to welcome you to our town. Is there anything I can do to assist you?'

'Thank you, I am Abdul Abdullah of Lahore and I have come here to do business,' said Diogenes, having memorised his identity papers.

'I see, I hope you will enjoy your stay and avoid this sort of trouble, what line of work are you in, if I may ask?'

''Well I am having some problems with one of your people who is not too keen on honouring his debts,' said Diogenes.

'I see. That is unfortunate, is there a large sum involved?'

'I am afraid there is.'

'I think I may be able to help here,' said Khalil.

'Oh really and how might that be?'

'Well in this area we have a ready supply of young people who, how can I put it, are willing make the ultimate sacrifice for the right price.'

'So, how would that work?' asked Diogenes.

'Simple, you pay us a small fee which includes the cost of the belts and we send two suicide bombers round, ready to do business with your debtor unless the money is paid. If the debtor refuses then they do the necessary,' explained Khalil.

'You mean they kill themselves. But what is in it for them and why are there two?' asked Diogenes.

'The two of them get eternal salvation, seventy two virgins etc. and you need two because one has to be a backup in case one of the devices fails,' said Khalil reassuringly.

18

Ingrid made her excuses and after a brief stop-over to collect her belongings she caught the first flight to Copenhagen.

Ingrid entered the Tivoli Gardens in the centre of Copenhagen in one of the few days when it wasn't raining. Tivoli was meant for children as a funfair but these days it was a mass of restaurants which purported to be from all over the world and spilled over into the paths between the flower arrangements and music. Her BlackBerry showed a text telling her that her father was waiting at the Café Morocco. It wasn't long before the enormous dome of pappi's head came into view reading *Politiken*, one of the most popular Danish newspapers. After several hugs the tears down pappi's cheeks told Ingrid that all was not right.

'Mommi is deteriorating rapidly, I am afraid, Ingrid,' said Pappi.

'When can we see her?' asked Ingrid.

'You can see her, but she has got to the stage where she is drifting in and out of a coma.'

'What do the doctors say?'

'Well I don't understand their jargon, I'm sure that you will, but they have told me that there is nothing to be done,' reported Pappi.

'I see, so how is Iceland Pappi, we all suffered with your volcano and with all the volcanologists at your university I am sure they could have told us a little earlier.'

'Yes, everyone is complaining there and what with the banks collapsing, I am wondering why I bothered to take the job there.'

'Still, I think we had better have something to eat and then go to see mommi,' suggested Ingrid who had eaten little since Syria.

It was a change to eat Gravad Lax and reindeer garnished with small boiled potatoes. Everything in Scandinavia was small and expensive and pay was heavily taxed and by the time the sales tax was added on, there was very little left. Mommi was in the specialised cancer hospital to the north of Copenhagen and it appeared that this was the intensive therapy unit by the number of tubes that emanated from her body. She had been a general practitioner in the central district of the city, and she covered the parliament and the international part of Denmark. Her eyes flickered and her body appeared to have suffered the ravages of the disease that was eating her away. After paying their respects, father and daughter shared a pot of coffee in the hospital canteen as a familiar face joined them. Inge was Ingrid's brother and had just arrived from New York. He was very tall and fair with his father's dome of a head.

'Is there any chance Ingrid?' asked Inge.

'I don't think so,' said Ingrid.

There was a pause as the air cleared and pappi left to pay his last respects, leaving sister and brother to catch up on each other's news. Ingrid received a text asking her to report to the Egyptian Embassy to help organise some loose ends. Inge shook his head.

'You are still busy saving lives, Ingrid and I hear that now you are saving them all over the world. Is it true that you are now the Egyptian Minister of Health?'

'And why shouldn't I be, Inge?'

'Absolutely, I have known for years that you would rule the world, so why not now,' said Inge.

'You can talk, you actually are ruling the world, what is it now, the Swedish envoy to the United Nations?'

'You are a little out of date my dear.'

'Sorry, what is it then?' asked Ingrid.

'Well it is little bit more international these days, just like you, but I do have some business for you, if you're not too busy.'

'Not too busy, you are joking, come on what is this?' said Ingrid.

'Well, a colleague of mine on one of the committees has developed a wasting disease that is taking over his body. It is in the early stages at present, but he is now largely in a wheelchair and I need his support for my projects and I promised I would ask you if you could help,' said Inge.

'Can you get him to Cairo?' asked Ingrid.

'That is not a problem; he is a Syrian by the name of al-Aleppo. I hear you are still knocking about with good old Freddie the engineer, how is he?'

'He is just fine and he is now the Minister of Defence just a few blocks away from me,' explained Ingrid.

'No I didn't mean that,' laughed Inge.

'I know what you meant and it's none of your business,' replied Ingrid.

Back in Egypt, Freddie was deep in discussion with Bill Stickleback, head of the Egyptian FBI/MI6 and espionage in general.

'What are we going to do about the Syrians, Bill?' asked Freddie.

'The same as we always do, go in, shake it all about and disappear.'

'But there are about twenty million of them,' pointed out Freddie.

'We don't need to bother most of them, just the ones who count,' said Bill.

'So that means the ruling party. I am assuming that they are quite happy with things as they are,' said Freddie.

'That can't carry on; things are changing and we aim to be the first ones in with our plans,' said Bill.

'I assume we are taking the CSA and some militia. How can we get them in?'

'The answer is Cyprus, it is close to Turkey and we can use Greek Cyprus as a holding area. We have to avoid using Turkey, as it is close to Syria and Iran, and Israel will not want to be involved,' explained Bill.

A message came through on Freddie's BlackBerry that a Mr al-Aleppo was waiting at the airport. He rang Ingrid for further instructions.

'I am going to have to see this chap,' said Ingrid.

'Why, what is this?' asked Freddie.

'He is a new challenge for us. Apparently he has some progressive nerve disease and my brother Inge, who asks after you, is a colleague of his,' said Ingrid.

'Are we doing these cases at the moment?' asked Freddie.

'There are other factors,' said Ingrid.

'And these are?'

'He is a Syrian at a high level, but also we haven't done a lot of this type of work, so we can learn things.'

'Just how much can we learn, I thought brains can only take in so much, like the hard drive on a computer?' asked Freddie.

Mr al-Aleppo was shown in to a suite down the corridor and given coffee and biscuits whilst technicians hooked him up to some system analysers. Samples were taken from various parts of his body before Freddie entered.

'I am honoured to see you doctor,' said al-Aleppo.

'Welcome to Cairo, Mr al-Aleppo I hope we can do something for you.'

'I hope so too, has Inge filled you in with my details?' asked al-Aleppo.

'Indeed he has and the rest will come from the test

that we are about to perform.'

'Thank you, I will do my utmost to co-operate with you and if there is any expense that is required do not hesitate to ask.'

'There will be no need for funds, sir. That is already taken care of,' said Freddie.

'I noticed on the way in that it is very much like home, I mean of course New York?' said al-Aleppo.

'Well, I thought you were aware that we are the first overseas state of the Confederate States of America, the Pyramid state, hopefully it is the beginning of a new world order.'

Ingrid's BlackBerry rang.

'Hi, Freddie, what can I do for you?'

'Do I remember something about a gentleman called al-Aleppo in an Israeli jail?' asked Freddie.

'Yes he's a real menace this guy, he specialises in IEDs and training suicide bombers. He is their chief ordinance officer. Why do you ask?'

'Because of the one here who is after an operation for a complex condition. Who is he, is he related?'

'They are a vast family that go back to Roman times. Some would say that they have been the real ruling class even when it was known as Assyria,' pointed out Ingrid.

Freddie was sifting through the test results and scribbling on a whiteboard that had been fastened on the walls of all the rooms on his orders.

'Where are we Freddie?' asked Ingrid.

'It looks like an LAR type problem although we need to do more live tissue work, to be sure. That could take years, we have to do replication studies and then clarify any risks before even phase two trials could begin,' explained Freddie.

'We don't have time for any of that,' said Ingrid. 'But we are dealing with patients who do not have that

much time and if we wait it may be too late anyway.'

Mr al-Aleppo was listening intently to the cutting-edge scientific discourse.

'Does that mean that I am a guinea pig?' he asked.

'Well not exactly,' said Freddie.

'Because I don't mind if I am. You just go ahead, I have nothing to lose.'

In the depths of Israel the Drohobyczerrebbe was at his weekly surgery doling out blessings, amulets and strategic advice. His headquarters were in a derelict shop that had been donated by a supporter for saving his family from pestilence. Amongst his followers was a rather shady small man in a pin-stripe suit together with a rather handsome tall muscular man with a worried look and some documents. This was the west bank of Jerusalem and such people were rare and stood out from the Palestinians, settlers and tourists. He handed the documents over to the rebbe who poured over the Aramaic script using a thick lens and rocking gently as he muttered to himself. The tall man spoke.

'I am from the Israeli security service and as you can see I have come across this document which needs to be shared with the Palestinians and I am authorised to negotiate on their behalf.'

''Can you fix this?' said Mamser, in his pin-stripe suit.

'We will make some contacts and come back to you,' said the rebbe.

19

'How can I get in touch with these people?' asked Diogenes.

'Don't you worry about a thing, my friend. I can fix all this for you,' said Khalil

'I just need to know a little more detail as my partners would not want anything to go wrong.'

'How can anything go wrong? I mean the two bombers go round, make sure we have the right guy and then bang.'

'And they get the salvation and my guy is obliterated and what about me?' asked Diogenes.

'Well he is not going to cause you problems, no more,' explained Khalil.

'But it does not help me as I have lost my money.'

'I see but you will cut your losses in eternity as your friend will not be able to steal money from anyone else.'

'I can see that, but I am a businessman and I deal in profits and losses and this is not going to go down so well with my bank manager. Maybe if you could put me in touch with the people who organise these bombers then I can try a more subtle approach,' said Diogenes.

Diogenes left with a name and address on the back of an empty packet of condoms and some vague directions through a maze of side streets. His peasant costume was beginning to decay so that it emitted a similar pungency to everyone else. After nearly an hour he began to realise that all the streets and alleyways looked much the same. He stopped at the Café Morocco for a rest and a single malt. The customers all looked similar superficially but that was only their ragged clothes. Their faces were of different colours from black via yellow to white. Some were Nubians, others Arabs and the rest Europeans. A minority looked frankly quite ill. He was the only one on the single malt; the rest were on Turkish coffee, Hookah and shots of cheap liquor. There seemed to be a never-ending line of customers entering the café to the extent that Diogenes wondered whether there was an exit so that they could re-enter in the same way as they wandered down the street. All were dressed in the same way except for the hats and some wore turbans; others favoured the fez and most had a keffiyeh. The robes were quite bulky to the extent that Diogenes could only guess whether there was an AK-47 beneath the cloak worn by the man who whispered some orders in his ear concerning the black Mercedes outside.

They quickly tied a cloth round his eyes and there was a dust cloud as they left the town and climbed up to a derelict house where he was pulled out of the car. At this stage the blindfold was removed and he found himself in a large hall with families and a sheikh on a chair at the front. The sheikh was chanting in Arabic. He spoke in a singing whining voice and rocked on his chair, only pausing from time to time to offer his hands, palm side up, to the ceiling. Diogenes was a fluent Arabic speaker and he also took in several other rather unfashionable languages at the time like Mandarin and Punjabi.

The sheikh had stopped chanting and was now talking of jihad. He beckoned forward all those who wished to be considered for the eternal sacrifice as he opened his arms. Immediately most of the people in the room came to him as if he was the pied piper beckoning the rats. Some of the helpers round the sides of the room had to forcibly restrain the crowd to prevent the sheikh being overrun.

'I can only take the true believers. You must take a

test to show him that you are fit for jihad,' announced the sheikh.

Diogenes was looking at his BlackBerry covertly whilst setting it to the co-ordinates that Professor Bi had worked out in conjunction with the experiment at the mental hospital, using the paranoid patients and the schizophrenics. The people in the room seemed to be showing rather different readings from those that he found in the mental hospital inmates. The test was supposed to try to distinguish which of the people in the room were the best candidates for jihad but the co-ordinates were all wrong. Diogenes knew that many of these people would volunteer for the supreme jihad and he also knew that you could buy suicide bombers to act as hit men for your enemies. What was happening was that it was normal people who were volunteering for suicide bombers, much like the Kamikaze pilots of old. The sheikh was addressing the crowd:

'I see many volunteers before me, but who are the most devoted? Some will do things to become popular but others will be the true martyrs and have their names venerated for all time. Which of you will make a video swearing allegiance to the holy jihad?'

The hordes still charged towards the sheikh with no sign of abating. The sheikh held up an old chipped jar and shook it about.

'In this jar are capsules of poison. Half of them are sweets and the others are poisonous but they all look the same. I want everyone who is ready for martyrdom to come forward and stand in line ready to take the risk.'

Diogenes took a call on his BlackBerry from Tamuz Halevy warning him to get out of the area. The sheikh was not happy that not all his followers were willing to take the pill test and he rounded on the non-believers.

'Why do you not join with us and make the supreme

sacrifice?' said the sheikh.

Nobody dared to answer but the ones who had volunteered became restless and were manhandling the others and beckoning them to join the martyrdom. Some of volunteers were larger than the others and made threats and were jostling them about. A rather large one rounded on Diogenes.

'Why do you not join with us?'

'Why should I?' said Diogenes.

'The sheikh says we have to make jihad and so we must do as he says.'

'No, you must do as he says, but I can do as I want.'

'So it doesn't make much difference either you kill me or the pill or the suicide bomb will kill me,' said Diogenes.

'We must not think of such things, we must have faith in the master and he will take care of us.'

Some of the other believers were gathering round Diogenes and beginning to detect a threat. The door burst open and a dozen military types with assault rifles burst in.

'What kept you?' asked Diogenes.

'The GPS was on the blink,' said Tamuz, from behind his camouflage mask.

'Look, I think we had better just round this lot up but it's important that we distinguish the ones who volunteered for the mission from the ones who did not,' said one of the militia.

'How about some orange tracksuits?' suggested Diogenes.

'But that would mean some of them were just left in their normal clothes: I think we need some form of tattoo that they couldn't remove,' said the militia man. 'I know; we have markers that we use to mark up hogs before they go to the slaughter house.'

Diogenes noticed that the militia were wearing

camouflage gear but their shoulder flashes were a lone star in red, white and blue. The motto "Free as a breeze, swift as a mustang" was inscribed under the name Texas Rangers, Confederate States of America. This was a skirmish group summoned to deal with a potentially tricky situation and after the tattooing the group were escorted to the awaiting helicopters. The terrain was quite rough and if it were not for the mouth gags and the twine binding their arms, there could have been complications.

It was a short hop to Cyprus where the prisoners were disembarked and split into different holding areas ready for debrief.

Diogenes received an email from Professor Bi. It read, "Good news, we have narrowed down the tests to distinguish the biological markers in the brains of the patients that you sent over. All we need is a blood sample now and we can divide the groups into normal, paranoid and schizophrenic."

Diogenes replied, "How about ones who have been brainwashed?"

The professor replied in the affirmative.

Diogenes went through his messages on the BlackBerry and realised that he couldn't afford the time to go personally to Geneva. After some preliminary washing and a change out of his rags, he arranged to be taken to the British embassy in Nicosia.

20

Mommi did not last until morning and after the funeral formalities, Ingrid caught the first plane to Cairo.

Ingrid was in her office in the ministry surfing the net for possibilities for Mr al-Aleppo when her phone rang.

'Hello this is the Drohobyczerrebbe; I have some news which may interest you.'

'Oh yes, rebbe,' said Ingrid.

'Indeed, I have what appears to be an authentic script in Aramaic, an ancient language spoken in the Middle East many years ago. This was brought to me by a man purporting to be from Mossad but I am not sure that he is aware of the consequences of the content of this document,' said the rebbe.

'How do you mean?' asked Ingrid.

'Well it is a historical tract dating back to biblical times and it is a description of the various people who occupy the Middle-Eastern territories.'

'So rebbe what does it say?'

'It clearly states that the Israelites or the Jews as we know them now, actually lived in Assyria which is the present day Syria and so the state of Israel, which the Zionists hold to be sacred, is in reality a falsehood,' explained the rebbe.

'So if this is the case, then the Jews, who want to be true to their ancient heritage, should really be in Syria,' said Ingrid.

'I am afraid that this is historically correct and there is other evidence for this. It is in the book of Micah but the Jews only read a fraction of this. I suppose it is an early case of redaction,' said the rebbe.

'So if we can gain control of Syria, then the Jews could move in if they wished and that would free Israel and solve the Middle East crisis,' said Ingrid with some trepidation.

Ingrid was writing down these ideas, but then had to excuse herself as Freddie was calling her to the laboratory.

'I think I have it, Ingrid,' exclaimed Freddie.

'Have what?' asked Ingrid.

'The answer to this chap from Syria, who joined us the other day, and his disease process.'

'Come on then, Freddie.'

'It is a glycoprotein that affects the myelinisation of the nerve sheaths,' announced Freddie.

'Does this help us?' asked Ingrid.

'I think it almost solves the problem because all we have to do is extract this chemical, break it down and analyse the defect in the patient, re-synthesize it and find a way of delivering it to the host, probably using stem cells.'

'As simple as that, then?' joked Ingrid.

'Absolutely, so clear off and by tea time I will have it ready. Oh by the way Bill Stickleback wanted you to pop in and have a chat,' said Freddie.

Bill Stickleback had a labyrinth of rooms in the basement and the CCTV was swivelling around following any heat source, so they could see you before you could see them. Ingrid was just walking around with no way of knowing how to find Bill or even to escape when a door opened and an electronic device ordered her to sit down on the only chair available. As she sat she was aware of an electronic laser type device passing over her from different angles of transmitters in the ceiling. A voice ordered her to move to the next room and stand on a cross marked in red. Finally a human in a suit opened a door, addressed her by name and took her into a large office with yet more surveillance devices. Bill Stickleback sat behind a semi-circular desk with a wad of print-outs. He boomed down to Ingrid taking advantage, not only of his height, but also of a raised platform.

'What's going on with the Syria Business?' demanded Bill.

'I think we need to move with this ASAP,' explained Ingrid.

'Why is that?' asked Bill.

'It's better you don't know that, but we might miss the opportunity if we delay,' said Ingrid.

'What opportunity?' asked Bill.

'As I said, the reasons will become apparent later, but if we can take Syria now, we will be on the front foot and it will be difficult for anyone else to act. I am aware that the CSA have some troopers in Greek Cyprus on another mission and so the logistics may be easier at present,' said Ingrid.

'What are they doing there?' asked Bill.

'Well, Cyprus is the new hot spot for world power. To put it simply the old world order was the USA, Russia, China and the Europeans. With the USA and European short of cash and war-weary and the Russians overstretched there is a void. Israel is the catalyst and needs to be watched. Cyprus is politically and geographically a key position as it has links with Greece and Turkey. In addition Turkey has not decided who to align itself with and could turn to Russia, Europe, the USA or even back to Israel and it is also close to Iran and Syria,' explained Ingrid.

'You have lost me a couple of minutes ago, can you try to summarise,' said Bill.

'Not really, because it is so fluid at the moment which is why we must seize the opportunity,' pointed out Ingrid.

'So what are you saying?' asked Bill.

'We have to go for Syria and use it to consolidate

our influence and I will contact the CSA bosses and tell them to reinforce, by the way is this going to have an effect on the CSA forces there already?' asked Ingrid.

'Ingrid, soon the CSA will be everywhere and no-one will notice. They are the new colonisers,' said Bill.

'So do we go to Greek or Turkish Cyprus?' asked Ingrid.

'I think we go in first with Special Forces and we can take the whole island and move on Syria. Who have you got in Syria?' asked Bill.

'Well I have a few contacts and I am just about to get another, but I will have to sort out a patient first, so give me a couple of days, otherwise Tamuz Halevy is a good first contact,' explained Ingrid.

The phone rang to say that Mr al-Aleppo was ready for treatment, which required Ingrid to find an exit from Stickleback's lair. It proved not as complex as finding her way in, as he accompanied her and his imprint seemed to open all the doors. In the treatment suite Freddie was waiting with a syringe full of straw coloured liquid marked "for intrathecal use". An assistant found a way into the spinal cavity and Ingrid slowly injected the thick liquid. She left her patient with a nurse who was to observe his vital signs on the monitors as she accompanied Freddie to his rooms.

Freddie's private accommodation was well hidden in the inner reaches of his office suite and he poured some Champagne cognac. Ingrid had peeled off her outer clothes to reveal underwear that had been hand-made by Lundquist of Copenhagen to her own design. The brassiere was the palest of blue, almost white, and the uplift was firm to compliment her natural breast structure. The end of the cups was delicately cut back so that her full nipple pushed itself through and could be emphasised under her blouse. Her panties were made of the same material but were along the lines of a

G string only with a hint of pink and revealed the deeper pink of her vulva. Freddie had filled the glasses when he caught a glimpse of her lying on the bed combing her hair and revealing her platinum jewellery with ornate filigree patterning. Freddie put down the drinks and pulled off his clothes to reveal his desire as Ingrid pulled him towards her. All other thoughts frittered away as they caressed each other and diverted their warmth towards the act. Ingrid spread her manicured fingers around his buttocks as she guided him inside once, twice and then in waves of penetration so deep, that they shook in unison and when the climax was near, there was only a brief pause until the whole process began again.

An intercom signalled that the nurse who was monitoring Mr al-Aleppo had a report for them.

'The patient is doing just fine and feels much more relaxed and is asking whether he can begin to mobilise but he has noticed a rather strange side effect.'

'What is that?' asked Ingrid.

'How can I put it, he seems to have an erection, which he has not experienced for some years. Oh yes and he would like to speak to you about something else as well as thanking you,' said the nurse.

Ingrid smiled and looked at Freddie as they switched off the sound and burst into hysterics. Ingrid tidied herself and returned to her office. Mr al-Aleppo was in his dressing gown and waiting for her as she entered.

'I must thank you for everything. I have to say that when Inge told me that you were the best I didn't think anyone could be that good. You have performed a miracle and miracles deserve that the recipient gives the miracle worker everything that he or she wants. I am ready to do what I can for you,' said al-Aleppo.

'I know that you are influential in your homeland,

but I also know that the situation there is far from stable which is a cause of much suffering to your people,' explained Ingrid. 'I am in touch with people who are trying to bring stability to the area and especially your own country but it may involve military intervention.'

'These are exactly my views, as Inge will tell you, and I have contacts there who can smooth the way for your people to enter. The ports of Latakia and Tartus are ideal for sea landings but may be well defended but the best way may be from the Turkish side. The Turks will be more disposed to help in Syria according to my international contacts and this could be useful for any incursions into Iran,' explained Mr al-Aleppo.

'So, do you feel that we can build up a force in Cyprus?' asked Ingrid.

'I could ask the Turks to invite you in to Turkish Cyprus, but use diplomatic contacts to offer financial aid to the Greeks so that they can't refuse especially if you guarantee not to invade Greek Cyprus and even act as peacemakers,' answered al-Aleppo.

'Have you heard about the idea that Assyria is the true home of the Jews?' asked Ingrid.

'Very much so, and there is an influential chap, whom I am sure you know, who has been saying that for years. Indeed his family goes back to biblical times,' replied Mr al-Aleppo.

'So, if I get you to liaise with our man, can you fix some contacts?' asked Ingrid.

'I regard this as my solemn duty, doctor.'

Ingrid's BlackBerry showed a message from General La Rochelle to contact him in Norfolk Virginia. Ingrid rang the contact number.

'Hello can I speak with General La Rochelle please, this is Sue Dakota?'

'Hello this is the office of the Marine Corps of Virginia, is this regarding a date with one of our enlisted men?' asked a female voice.

'Not exactly it is another matter,' said Ingrid.

'The general is a busy man and does not trouble himself with popular singers, so I need to know what it is exactly that you want.'

'Look ma'am it was he who asked me to make contact, so I would be obliged if you could give him the message that I am on the line,' explained Ingrid.

'This is very irregular, y'know; my job could be on the line here,' said the voice.

'I think you will find that if you don't put me through, you will be on the line,' said Ingrid.

'General La Rochelle here, that is Sue I presume,' said the BlackBerry.

'It is indeed, what can I do for you?' asked Ingrid in the persona of Sue Dakota.

'Well I am getting a few confused messages here. We are about to send a force to Turkish Cyprus but we have also responded to a call to send men to Greek Cyprus. This looks like World War Three in the making.'

'Well general, I have not been involved in the Greek bit, can you tell me a bit about that?'

'It's a bit muddled, but it is linked with suicide bombers, are you involved here?' asked the general.

'Certainly not,' said Sue.

'So you don't know a character called Tamuz Halevy?' asked the general.

21

Diogenes managed to catch the last plane to London and it was 9pm when he rang the bell at Marie's apartment. He had decided to spend some time doing lab work rather than jet set in and out of zones that were dedicated to killing him. A click told him that Marie had activated the door lock and he was able to go through to her lounge. She was looking out of the window across some parks and Diogenes could see that she was wearing no clothes. As he moved towards her she turned round to a profile position holding a glass of wine. She was petite with brown hair that curled forward around the level of her ears and was short at the nape of her neck. Around her neck was a delicate gold chain that matched her pendant earrings and drew attention to her delicate neck and her pert, almost pubescent nipples. She was pale with a hint of the sun and as his eyes fixed on her body, he noticed that her tuft was compact and inviting. Her slim legs were not those of an athlete but more the type that a schoolgirl might need to lay on a warm rug in the winter.

Diogenes had travelled in smart casual so as not to delay his flight and cause disruption, and his diplomatic status helped him to get away from the airport soon enough to see Marie at her most desirable. She poured him some wine, kissed him just once on the lips and gently pretended to nudge him. It had been a long time gathering pace, but that was what made it so sensual, and as they caressed, she thrust the body part that needed attention to his lips and sighed in a heightened crescendo that suggested more was needed. In between, her delicate pale hands manoeuvred his clothes to the degree of undress that she needed to complete her task. Their lovemaking soon developed into a rhythm of heightened crescendos that found them on the floor. It was a signal to make a dive into the bedroom where Marie was soon astride him. It was like a French takeaway in bed with wine and it was the perfect combination to end weeks of concentrated brain sapping creativity.

The next day in the laboratory, Marie was gathering her data and preparing a PowerPoint presentation to bring Diogenes back to speed with their last meeting.

'As I understand it, the piece of tissue was from the brain of a failed suicide bomber?' said Marie.

'It was, but there were two problems: firstly I was hoping that this was a sample from the temporoparietal region,' replied Diogenes.

'And the second one?' asked Marie.

'Well the second gives rise to a third one in that the bomber had already been neutralised using a low frequency x-ray, which could compromise the results, and a third one is that we do not yet know whether this is an optimum area of the brain to be looking for solutions.'

'Well here are the topographical studies on the sample you supplied. As you can see there is a large area of obliteration stretching from the median pre-frontal cortex to the latero-occipto-cortex,' pointed out Marie.

'Did you look at the firing of neurones in these areas?' asked Diogenes.

'Well, as the tissue was dead, albeit in a preserving fluid, we were reduced to looking at preserved cells, but I think you need to find a more sophisticated fixing agent or else try to get hold of in vivo tissue and I think it is going to be difficult to get consent to take live samples,' pointed out Marie.

'Oh I don't know about that,' said Diogenes, laughing.

Marie smiled as she cleared her throat. Diogenes told her about his Cyprus project and Professor Bi's assertion that blood samples could be used as a marker for these changes.

'I can't see how we can link any blood elements, even at the most advanced level of analysis, that could act as markers without the backup of living tissue,' said Marie.

'And even if we could, the problem of how to manipulate the results of the analysis so as to affect change seems the stuff of dreams,' said Diogenes.

Marie drew an expansive multi-colour diagram on a whiteboard but there were just too many question marks and blanks. Diogenes received a text message from Professor Bi.

"I think that I may have something here that may be of interest. There are some patterns emerging in the blood samples that show some differentiation. Could you get some live brain samples from the same cohort of people?" asked Professor Bi.

Diogenes turned to Marie:

'I knew we would get to this. How on earth do we get a live brain sample organised?'

'What's your problem?' asked Marie.

'My problem, where do I start?'

'Is it true to say the sample you sent came from Central America?' asked Marie.

'I couldn't possibly comment,' replied Diogenes.

'And is it true to say that the rest of your detainees are at a secret location?'

'I couldn't possibly comment.'

'So from your observations I gather, that if we moved group one to location two, then no-one knows and then we can do anything,' observed Marie.

'I couldn't --------' said Diogenes. 'OK, I'll pull some strings. Do I take it that you are up for this?'

Mordechai McIntyre, literary agent, was in his usual seat in the Nelson's Column public house. The noise was a constant cacophony of public school obscenity concerning toilets and hysterical laughter. Mordechai was always alone, embedded in heaps of manuscripts and there was little room for anyone else at his table and this suited him perfectly as he was in a different world from the rest. Some had tried to steal his seat in the past but his lack of deodorant and dishevelled suit in the style of a nineteenth-century dandy, with a large gut protruding from his waistcoat, had the effect of repelling all invaders.

'Ah, here I will make room for you. I thought they had finally finished you off, it is a long time, I'm glad you've come because I was getting worried,' said Mordechai.

'Oh that's very touching I didn't think you cared,' said Diogenes.

'Oh, not about you, about your story, old boy. Don't you think an academic publisher of nano-whatever might be more appropriate for this story?' asked Mordechai.

'What makes you think of scientific publishers?'

'Well this is cutting edge research and if you trim out the characters you could have a chair in Cambridge or a directorship in a lucrative chemical company,' suggested Mordechai, with tongue in cheek.

'Trim out the characters; they are the story, and anyway it's fictional,' said an angry Diogenes.

'Fictional, last time we met you threatened to extinguish part of my brain,' pointed out Mordechai.

'They do sound a little two-dimensional though, I do admit,' agreed Diogenes.

'Well the main characters are spies so there has to be some mystery about their characters and the rest of them move in rather obscure circles, so they will be rather shady,' said Mordechai. 'But where are they going and why is it important that they get there?'

'I can assure you that the existence of the planet as we know it depends on their missions, so the book could not be more vital to our welfare,' said Diogenes.

'Yet it is fictional, though old boy.'

'Exactly, that is my point but I didn't say which parts are fictional and to what degree it is fictional.'

'You are worrying me now,' said Mordechai.

Diogenes's BlackBerry was summoning him to the Café Morocco in the West End of London, where he was to meet a man in an NY baseball cap and a Crombie. He made his excuses and left Mordechai as confused as ever but with a smile on his face.

'I am going to need a way into the world of suicide bombers and a contact who is trustworthy and committed,' said Diogenes.

'I know the one for you, what sort of skills should this person have?' asked Leonardo.

'I can deal with that, but we need integrity and speed, someone who is respected at an international level a clean skin but of high intellect,' announced Diogenes.

'Where are you going to be next?' asked Leonardo.

'I will let you know, but I will need your help to get there either overtly or otherwise.'

'You mean an undercover travel agent?' asked Leonardo.

'You could say that,' said Diogenes.

'I will tell you electronically in the next few days,' said Leonardo as he left the café.

Diogenes arrived at Geneva International Airport that evening and headed towards an airport hotel and a long bath with a bottle of single malt from the duty-free shop. It had been a long day and much had been achieved except there was nothing tangible on the route to his primary goal of controlling people's minds electronically or, even at this stage, making any watertight connections between brain structures and their thought processes. Perhaps Mordechai was right, maybe his literary world was more in touch with reality than Diogenes's scientific world.

Professor Bi on the other hand could not be more detached from the world around him. Diogenes was surprised that he ever left his laboratory either to eat or sleep, but over the years they had trained him to keep body and soul together and, when Diogenes burst through the door, he was not surprised to see him prone on a mat pointing towards a small table with trinkets dangling from plastic trees. Diogenes had been in the room about two minutes before Bi rose mumbling and noticed his visitor.

'Ah welcome back, do take a seat, I have some science for us to absorb and maybe you have something for me too eh?' said Professor Bi.

'I certainly hope so there is much to do and so much rides on this,' said Diogenes.

'Ah I see, let's start then,' said the professor.

22

Ingrid was getting immersed in international politics without realising it and she saw that the largest risk was that the USA may get precipitated into another civil war. Ingrid rang her contact in the Arab League to test out some hypotheses.

'This is Ingrid; can you put me through to your foreign minister please?'

'Hello, this is the personal assistant to the prince, what can I do for you?'

'I was hoping to either meet up with him or have a chat,' said Ingrid.

'Can you tell me what this is about?' asked the PA.

'Well I can't really; it's a bit of a delicate matter.'

'The prince is a busy man and I need to know some more about your business before I can disturb him,' pointed out the PA.

The prince was seated in an enormous office with high ceilings with stucco whorls in various shades of pale green. The furniture was ornate and possibly dated back to the days of the caliphate. Tables were laden with fruits and pastries and the prince was chewing and surfing the internet whilst drinking Turkish coffee in his inner sanctum. In the corner was a Nubian in flowing Arab dress fast asleep on a large settee. Outside the office there were two sentries in a uniform that was a hybrid between the modern army and the Moorish invaders of the middle ages. They carried Kalashnikov rifles and in their belts were scimitars and they were smoking cheroots as they sat on hard wooden chairs and dozed. Ingrid was bored with riddles and the PA on the telephone and had simply walked down the road, flashed her government pass and entered the prince's office unseen whilst the guards dozed. She sat in one of the armchairs and cleared her throat until the prince noticed her.

'I think your security arrangements need some overhaul, your highness,' said Ingrid.

'Ah Ingrid, for you there is no need, you are always welcome, my house, your house, as they say,' said the prince with a welcoming smile.

'I think we need to talk politics,' said Ingrid.

'Politics, that is not one of my strong points, have you tried the Egyptian politicians?' inquired the prince.

'It is Arab politics that I am interested in. We seem to have Egypt under control as you know, but we may have some difficulties with a few of the others,' pointed out Ingrid.

'Only a few of them, you surprise me, I would have thought that all of our members disagree about everything and indeed it is from this diversity that we draw our strength,' said the prince.

Ingrid had some problems with this logic, but in her short tenure as Minister of Health she had become aware of the hours wasted in lengthy discourse about even trivial matters. She was aware that the divide and rule philosophy was universally accepted and, although the prince almost certainly was also aware of this, he rapidly used his mouse to change his computer screen from topless nymphets to Arabic policy documents.

'I am sure you are aware of the Syrian problem, prince, but matters have become rather urgent and may spill over to the rest of your members,' pointed out Ingrid.

'Our members seem to be obsessed with Israel and oil revenue and I am not sure that a few thousand refugees moving territories would be of much interest as the Arabs have been Bedouins for millennia. So what is it that you propose?' inquired the prince yawning.

'We want your backing or at least your neutrality over our proposal to invade Syria and establish a similar situation to here.'

'Not a problem, at present Syria is suspended from the Arab League and so we have no jurisdiction there. Furthermore, hardly anyone has strong ties with the country and even then it is linked to oil. There are plenty of our members who would be only too happy to chip in with a few extra barrels to make up for the shortfall and no-one would want to give any military aid and get drawn into a war,' answered the prince.

'So we have your blessing, your highness?'

'I couldn't possibly comment,' replied the prince.

Ingrid moved back into her office with Mr al-Aleppo, now fully recovered. 'The only difficulty we have now is the United Nations and the USA, Mr al-Aleppo.'

'I can lobby the UN with the help of Inge and with the Arab League on board, apart from a few rogue states, who do not have the veto, I can't see any problem,' said al-Aleppo.

'But what about China and Russia?' asked Ingrid.

'They would only be interested if their trade was affected or it was a neighbouring territory and although they may huff and puff only the fact that the USA would be split would be of great interest to them,' said al-Aleppo.

'So we are back to the USA?' said Ingrid.

'I am afraid we are, you will have to go over there Ingrid.'

A text message came through from T-Bone Redneck. "How y'all doin' Sue. How's about you coming over for the gig of all gigs. You just can't miss this one."

Ingrid was probably the only Egyptian minister to fly into Nashville via Sweden where she picked up her guitar. Chuck and T-Bone were in the hotel bar in downtown Nashville to welcome her. The table was heaving under the weight of Budweisers, and the rest of the clientele were at best semi-conscious.

'Why have you dragged me all the way over from the Middle East, boys?' asked Ingrid.

'You will not be disappointed, Sue, this is the biggie of all biggies,' said Chuck.

'It's not another night club with about thirty people eating burgers piled high with a choice of seven sauces and a mountain of fries?' asked Ingrid.

'Not quite; this is none other than the First Lady's gig, at the White House, a cosy soiree, with only the top country artists, cocktails and canapés,' said T-Bone.

The next day they were transported in a presidential limo past all the marines to the East Room at the White House.

The First Lady explained that it was part of her initiative to bring together indigenous country music unique to the USA. The East Room was the venue where not only the established musicians like Sue Dakota and T-Bone Redneck could come together, but also some aspiring artists, so that they could gel and show off the best of the best. The First Lady said that although Washington DC was not recognised as the origin of the genre, these days artists were as likely to hail from New York as New Orleans. Even foreigners had muscled in on the act, with Canada and Australia supplying some of the top bands. As the concert progressed the president and their children could be seen to squeeze in at the back of the room tapping their feet and swaying to the music. The First Lady was more than enthusiastic, and after the show over drinks she introduced Sue Dakota to the president.

'I really enjoyed your music and I gather that is only one of your many talents, Sue,' said the president.

'Well I wouldn't be so bold Mr President,' answered Sue.

'I have been briefed about your surgical skills and your Middle-Eastern efforts.'

'I hope I am not treading on any toes there,' said Sue with some trepidation.

'Not at all, the Middle East is a real pain, I lay awake at night worrying about that place and now with so many uprisings, it seems to be worse rather than better,' said the president.

Sue was unsure as to how much he knew about the Confederate states situation and whether he was for it or against it. Now was the pivotal moment that could make or break the whole exercise and she was the one who could take this responsibility.

'Do you mind if I ask you a favour, Sue?' asked the president.

'Why yes, I mean fire away, if I can help you in any way,' said Sue.

'The First Lady has an uncle of whom we are all very proud. He won a Silver Star in Vietnam along with his Purple Heart. Unfortunately his wounds have severely limited his activities and more recently he has been in so much pain that he has been begging the doctors for euthanasia. None of us would want this for such a brave veteran and I just wondered whether you could offer an opinion about what we should do next.'

'Well I can't guarantee that I can change things, but I will certainly have a look at him if that is OK,' said Sue.

'OK I will have him sent up tomorrow and you can have a look, give him a check-up and let us know what you think,' said the president.

Sue spent a restless night in the White House feeling like a mole sent to spy on the largest superpower of all. She rang Freddie for a catch up.

'How are we doing Freddie?'

'Well things are at a standstill. I've had this gent called Tamuz Halevy on the phone asking to come over. He's very persuasive but wants to help in any way he can. It seems he needs us to invade Syria more than anything and he often had to break off from his conversation due to gunfire or explosions in the background. I have agreed to see him this afternoon, although I am at a loss as to how he will manage to get out of Syria in one piece,' said Freddie.

'How much do you know about him?'

'I asked Bill to check him out but whenever you find a lead it seems to fizzle out and you get diverted up another blind alley. But one thing is sure, there are quite a few links with another shadowy figure called Mamser Ha-erev who wanders about Israel. Have you heard of these guys?'

'I am afraid not, but I do know the President of the USA.'

'You mean someone who believes he is President of the USA?' asked Freddie.

'No, this is for real, and we may be able to help him with a little problem,' pointed out Ingrid.

Ingrid rang off as she heard some clicking on the line and a flunky signalled that they were ready for her. Sue was chauffeur-driven to a mansion in a large estate that was surrounded by shifty, lean men with wires coming out of their ears. Each one seemed to possess a neck that swivelled around nearly 360 degrees. She was led past guards through a succession of rooms to a bedchamber and some clinicians in white coats. An elderly physician sat her down to explain the case.

'I am sorry to have brought you all this way but the First Lady felt that you were the last hope.'

'My pleasure, sir,' said Ingrid.

'Well here you see Ralph; he was in Vietnam and he

was captured by the Vietcong and lined up to be executed. He was facing a wall and the firing squad took aim and he was hit by a single bullet in the back of the neck. He fell to the ground and they left him for dead with the others. Fortunately he was alive and in time he came round and was rescued by the advancing US infantry. He appeared to just have a skin wound but as time went by he lost the use of his lower limbs and he was taken to a Veteran's hospital. They found that the bullet had become diverted downwards in the spinal canal but they were reluctant to intervene in case he developed full-blown paralysis. So he was sent home with a care package and all was well, until recently, when after a fall he started to deteriorate. At the moment he has become paralysed but it is increasing and the fear is that soon he will be totally dependent,' explained the physician.

Ingrid examined the patient with some care, testing reflexes and looking at the scans already performed.

She texted Freddie: "Hi Freddie, do you remember the little problem I mentioned, well it's more complex than I thought. We have a wandering bullet in the spinal canal that not only needs stopping but also we need to try to reverse the damage it has done."

23

The case was much more complicated because Diogenes had to deal with a possible case of distinguishing one suicide bomber in a crowd, any of whom may be the bomber. Even more, he had to not only identify the bomber, but also quickly work to neutralise the bomb. Then he had only one brief moment to detonate the device and to destroy the brain of the bomber. So detection and neutralisation had to be instantaneous.

'You've heard of the Milgram experiment from the nineteen sixties?' asked Bi.

'Remind me,' challenged Diogenes.

'It was in all the basic psychology textbooks,' pointed out Bi.

'Not the sort of education I had, professor.'

'OK, a quick recap. A psychologist called Milgram got a group of students in a room and instructed them on how to use a machine that delivered electric shocks to people in the next room. They would be asked to gradually increase the intensity of the shocks from low to high on the instructions of a man in a white coat. As the shocks were increased, the pain of the people in the next room could be heard by the one who delivered the shocks,' explained Bi.

'So what did that prove?' asked Diogenes.

'The results showed that some of the ones delivering the shocks were prepared to increase the intensity of the shocks right to the highest level, whereas others would not, and stopped at various stages.'

'So some of them were oblivious to the damage they were doing to the others,' said Diogenes.

'That's right.'

'But what happened to the ones who were severely

shocked, and was this ethical?'

'Absolutely, it was ethical and no-one was hurt.'

'You mean this was all fabricated.'

'Exactly,' said Bi.

'So how is this relevant to my problem?'

'Well it shows, just like you have, that some people are more easily brainwashed than others,' explained Bi.

'But we know this.'

'We do, but in order to replicate the findings I had to use this scenario, but at the same time attach the volunteers to brain scanning equipment and I also had to slightly change the format in case they knew about Milgram.'

'So what did you find?'

'Well we used SPECT scanners and we noticed a differentiation in the insula and the anterior cingulate cortex of the brain,' pointed out Bi.

'Interesting, but did you look into this further?'

'Indeed, we used scans labelled with various tracers and the one that seemed to correlate mostly with the different groups was the glutamate one.'

'So it is glutamate control in these areas that is the key.'

'Correct,' said Bi.

'Have you got any ideas on how to alter the glutamate affinity?' asked Diogenes.

'Isn't that enough? After all I am primarily a nanochemist so you need a nanopharmacotherapist for that,' snapped Bi. 'You could try Professor Schweinfurtel, he is linked with the military.'

Diogenes moved down the corridor to a door marked "Prof. Schweinfurtel, Chemist." He was about to knock on the door when a voice chimed out 'Ring the Bell'.

As his finger neared the bell the door opened and another voice beckoned him to sit down and wait. The room was 100% white and Schweinfurtel was as white as the surroundings, which made him hardly visible except for his teeth that were yellow. This had the effect of unnerving the visitor who could not see Schweinfurtel.

'I am looking at influencing glutamate receptors,' announced Diogenes.

'Influencing them?' queried Schweinfurtel.

'Yes, we are on the brink of identifying them in some brain tissue and as soon as we have achieved that we need to neutralise or modify them,' explained Diogenes.

'And how do you think we can help you with this?' asked Schweinfurtel.

Diogenes stood up and picked one of the marker pens from the shelf below the whiteboard. Immediately the professor shot out of his chair to prevent Diogenes touching the marker pen.

'Please do not touch this. Put on these white gloves and tell me what you want to write and I can do it,' said Schweinfurtel in some haste.

'How can I tell you that when I am not sure myself until I start the train of thought?' asked Diogenes.

'Well, let's just talk about it without touching anything and wear this face mask so that you do not breathe on anything,' said Schweinfurtel, getting fidgety.

Diogenes appeared rather puzzled as the professor brushed his white tunic down in an alcove in the far corner of the room. There was a white table and a white bin operated by his foot nearby. Diogenes sat immobile watching these actions and wondering how he was going to escape.

'As I was saying, we are interested in how the military might be able to detect and control the glutamate receptors in the insula and the anterior cingulate gyrus.'

The professor looked puzzled as he cleaned down his computer and tried to operate the keyboard and the mouse wearing his white gloves.

'I do not remember reading about this, what are your references?' asked Schweinfurtel.

'Well I was hoping to take you through this before you stopped me using the whiteboard,' explained Diogenes.

The professor was glancing around the room in a state of anxiety and seemed at a loss for words as he took to rocking in his white chair and making purring noises. Diogenes took his chance and extracted himself from the chair and the whiteness, flung open the door and took a deep sigh of relief as he tripped over Professor Bi.

'You look like you've seen a ghost,' said Bi.

Diogenes smiled weakly as he staggered down the corridor, followed by the Chinese scientist, and sat in Bi's office breathing heavily.

'I guess I was right then,' said Bi.

'You could have warned me. Is he always like that?'

'Not when he leaves his office, he is a little like an animal marking his territory.'

'Is there anyone else you can recommend?'

'Actually there is, in Stanford, California, there is a charming lady who has the chair in brain physiology. I think you may get some more help there,' announced Bi as he wrote her email address on a card.

Diogenes smiled, he was just happy to have escaped intact from the white laboratory. His BlackBerry told him to head for London and after a short taxi ride to the airport he helped himself to a single malt in the executive lounge.

His first appointment was in a Whitehall department.

'Can you tell us how much progress you have made with the project?' asked Leonardo.

'It is difficult to be specific at this stage and it has become rather more technical than I thought it would be,' explained Diogenes.

'Don't worry, in this department we spend all our time devising hyper-technical ideas for our national needs.'

'OK, we are looking to detect and modify glutamate receptors in specific parts of the brain,' explained Diogenes.

'How far have you got?' asked Lenardo.

'I have a man in Geneva and a lady in the USA who may be able to link up these stages and then I have to make this operational and we can start the trials.'

'So this will be the suicide bombers dealt with. How far along are you with the IDE problem?' asked Leonardo.

'That is in production as we speak,' said Diogenes.

'Good, very good. The next stage is the political one, so I will move you to the other section,' said Leonardo, as he pressed a button.

'Thank you for joining us today. I thought I would bring you up to speed with the political dimension. Times they are a changing on the world picture. We used to be at the top table, but the Berlin wall came down, the USA became overstretched and Europe was overloaded with poor nations on the fringes who bled them dry,' explained the senior mandarin.

'So how does that affect us?' asked Diogenes.

'I don't know at this time, but I think we need to be pre-emptive, sooner rather than later.'

'So why are you telling me this?' asked Diogenes.

'Because I am aware that there are moves to split the USA and incorporate many or all of the Arab states into what used to be called the Confederate states of

America and that is why we have selected yourself and some of the top brains for this task,' explained the mandarin.

There was a text message on Diogenes's BlackBerry: "Can you head over to Stanford. I think that we have progress on glutamate physiology that may prove to be the link that we have been seeking. Professor Bi has filled me in on the mechanics and the sooner we start the better".

'Something new?' asked the mandarin.

'I guess you could say so, but I need to get the first flight over the pond,' explained Diogenes.

24

In Cairo Freddie was deep in conversation with Bill and Carlo about the increasing need for security with the growing empire of Confederate states. They had a map of Syria on the wall and they were using marker pens to divide territories. When one territory was marked B for Bill, Carlo chopped off a strategic bit and marked it C.

'What difference does it make, can't you just sort this out when we get there?' said Freddie.

'It doesn't work like that, old boy. We need to have as much in place as we can beforehand otherwise we get a civil war,' said Bill.

Freddie went back into his laboratory, fished out a few rats and scribbled some equations on a whiteboard as he selected relevant chemicals that would help Ingrid with her latest conundrum. Fiddling with complex scientific equipment, and the challenge of putting together the science behind it, was what gave him a thrill.

Ingrid wanted to be able to replace nervous tissue and prevent more destruction of it. Freddie saw this as two distinct stages of work. The first was to cleanse the nerves and make sure the destructive process could not set in again, and the second was to either regenerate or re-create the nervous tissue. He worked quickly as he anaesthetised the rats and exposed their sciatic nerves. The idea was that he would try to simulate the condition of Ingrid's patient and then test out remedies on the rats. He proceeded to cut the nerves and let them settle, whilst he tinkered with his chemicals. He had a collection of rats with nerve damage and he was cleansing debris to prepare for any grafting, so as to make sure it did not damage the new nerve tissue. Work like this was necessarily slow, as duplication was needed, and you had to be sure that the experiment could be replicated without problems.

Ingrid, on the other hand, was short of time and the rat experiments were not going fast enough and, as much as Freddie wanted the extracts to aid the conduction in the nerves, he only saw some minimal muscle twitching. Ingrid was texting him to enquire about the progress and he knew that he had to try something, to at least delay the disease process.

The patient joked with Ingrid and his sister, the First Lady. The patients always told Ingrid that they had come out of desperation and would understand if nothing could be done, but Ingrid had an inner drive that meant that the less they expected, the more she would strive to find something. Since childhood she had always striven to be the best in everything and, apart from a brief period, when she strove to be thinner than everyone else, she had succeeded. The doctors and the psychologists had explained that she had low self-esteem at that time, despite her achievements, but that was enough to jolt her out of the cycle which peaked when she married a billionaire. Miles, her ex-husband, had been lucky enough to inherit large swathes of Texas, and the resultant oil and other spin-offs had been enough to make sure that Ingrid never needed to work again as she settled into her manor house in its grounds about the size of Denmark. She rapidly became the envy of all the wives in her social circle whilst Miles travelled the world making contacts.

But Ingrid was waiting for the opportunity to treat her VIP patient and Freddie was not forthcoming with the material. She texted him, "Hi Freddie, any chance of that nerve replacement kit coming over here?"

Carlo meanwhile had his own worries and as Freddie was reading the text he knocked and entered the laboratory.

'Hey Freddie what you got in here, you making a new A-bomb?'

'Can't you see I am in the middle of something urgent? What do you want?' asked Freddie.

'Well it's like this boss, what with us going in to this new country Surreya; I need to touch base with the organisation, so we can get everything in place so to speak,' said Carlo.

'It's Syria actually, and yes, I can see that, but you can do me a favour when you go over.'

'Anything at all boss, whatever you say.'

'Right, I want you to take this packet to Ingrid who is in Washington DC as soon as you get there; maybe fly direct if you can,' requested Freddie.

What Freddie had not factored in, was the reception Carlo might get as he entered the Homeland security at Dulles airport Washington. His name was on a list from some years back when he was involved in a drugs bust. There was a lot of interest in his package, from everyone except the sniffer dogs, and this made him even more of a suspect.

Ingrid soon got to know about this via Freddie who was hopping mad at the delay and the possibility of the chemicals being contaminated. At the same time there was a phone call from Ingrid's ex-husband.

'Hi Ing, it's me Miles, I hear you're in DC, is there a chance we could hook up if you've got time?'

'Really Miles what a time to ring, just when I'm elbow deep in someone's back, what is it you want?' asked Ingrid.

'Oh nothing, it's just that I'm still a senator, I'm up in DC a lot and long time no see.'

'Well actually Miles there are a few things. Could you pop by now?' asked Ingrid.

Miles was only down the corridor and they were able to meet in an anti-room. It had been a short tempestuous marriage interrupted by affairs on both sides. They were tipped to be presidential candidate and First Lady, but Miles was seen as a loose cannon and not to be trusted with levels of state, and as that chance disappeared their marriage seemed to disintegrate and Freddie was in the background.

'Miles, there is a rather urgent matter which maybe you could help solve. There is a chap called Carlo, who is being detained in Homeland Security here in DC, and he has a parcel that I need urgently for my patient, who is the First Lady's brother.'

'Ingrid, take it as done,' said Miles.

Miles deftly pressed about a dozen numbers on his cell phone.

'Hi this is Senator Di Angelo, I believe you have a certain Carlo with you at DC airport?'

'What of it sir?'

'Well, I have it from the highest level that he is needed at the White House ASAP, can you fix that?' ordered Miles.

'Let me check this, can you just hang on.'

Miles exchanged pleasantries with Ingrid revealing that he was now happily re-married with two children and lived in Dallas and when he was not in the senate, he was a federal judge.

'Senator, are you aware that this gentleman has a long record, and also we believe him to have links to the Mafia?' said the security officer.

'I am led to believe that he is a US citizen and as such he is subject to the fifteenth amendment,' announced the senator.

'Well I can't deny that. But he has a package which we believe may contain illicit drugs.'

'You believe, does it or doesn't it?' asked Miles.

'Well, my staff is in the process of analysing this.'

'How long is this going to take? I am here at the

White House where a doctor is waiting for this packet so that she can urgently treat a member of staff at the highest level. Do you want me to inform them that you have blocked this whilst you wait for it to be analysed?' said Miles.

'Well listen senator, I am not actually blocking this I am just being a loyal patriot and protecting the Homeland for all of us,' explained the officer.

Miles was not a patient man and when he heard civil servants bullshitting to save their skins he had difficulty retaining control, but his ex-wife had heard this many times and she intervened.

'I am the doctor involved here,' she interjected. 'And it is urgent that we get this material. If you want to know what it is I can tell you it is a glutamic acid derivative and there should be a minute battery and wire in the package. It is harmless but the patient here is deteriorating and this is at the highest level of security. Carlo, the gentleman who has delivered the material, is working with me abroad and as such he is subject to diplomatic immunity as well as being a US citizen. Can you send the package here as soon as possible please?'

Ingrid turned to Miles.

'Many thanks for that, I won't forget it. Can you just hang on until I finish the procedure and then maybe we could catch up over lunch?'

25

Sitting in business class en route to LAX was enough for tension to build in Diogenes's head. He knew that the only certain cure was whisky, and luckily the drinking could begin as soon as he was seated, and it was just as well, as the tight band around his head was becoming so painful that he was feeling nauseous, and the back of his neck was aching. He knew that the next pain was going to be in his teeth and there were many quack dentists who had tried to persuade him to have them all removed.

The disembarkation at Los Angeles was a form of detox. And on leaving the aircraft he caught a taxi to the department of brain physiology. It was all glass and steel with an open-plan design and groups of white-coated scientists furiously scribbling on plastic boards in between dashing to animal experiments. A small Gallic-looking girl emerged from the complex to welcome him.

'Hi, I'm Cherie,' she announced.

'I was told that you know about nano-receptors of glutamate,' said Diogenes.

'Well I know a bit, come with me and I'll show you where we are at.'

Cherie led Diogenes through a succession of secure rooms using her coded pass to a laboratory that was a mixture of what looked like a chemistry set, a collection of twig-like, odd shaped multi-colour structures, and a bank of computers.

'We have been working on glutamate detection for the last few years and by using FRET or Fluorescence Resonance Energy Transfer we have been able to measure them more accurately than before,' said Cherie.

'I am interested in measuring high density of glutamate in certain areas of the brain in an easily detectable manner, but using a form of equipment that could be used by a trained operative and deliver the result in seconds. Is that possible?' asked Diogenes.

Cherie went back to her computers and to some pre-rigged experimental material whilst she adjusted wires and took readings which she typed on to the computer. Whilst she was doing this Diogenes was communicating with Marie in preparation for a trip back to London. He received a text message: "I heard that you were in the US of A. Can you meet me in San Diego urgently about your book. We may be into something big here. Mordechai".

Diogenes told Marie about the delay, but he knew that she would understand. Diogenes received another text from Tamuz Halevy inquiring about what plans he had for the group of experimental volunteers that were waiting for further orders, in Cyprus.

'Cherie, have you any idea how long it will take for you to find a solution to this problem?' asked Diogenes.

'Can't say at present but I will need my team to work full out on this. Do you have any funding source?' asked Cherie.

'Let me just say the Arab league is more than generous and has instructed me just to send them the bill.'

Diogenes left Cherie and caught a shuttle to San Diego where Mordechai McIntyre was there to welcome him and transport him to a hotel with a bar in the Gaslight District. Mordechai arranged for a triple shot of single malt to sooth Diogenes's rising pain whilst he rummaged through a heap of papers in his briefcase.

'Glad you could make it, I thought I would catch

you out here for the annual film festival,' said Mordechai.

'Film festival, couldn't I just have gone to the movies, why do I have to come here?' asked Diogenes.

Mordechai was taking his time and the table was looking quite precarious as drinks were balanced on the edge. He fished out a yellowing dog-eared heap with a wry smile and announced that tomorrow was the day when it would be happening. Diogenes looked puzzled but calm as he focussed on his own manuscript. The atmosphere was filled with video screens and the noise of either baseball, American football or the latest Pop Idol.

'Tomorrow,' announced Mordechai. 'We shall pitch your book to about twenty movie producers and hope that one will bite and propel us to stardom.'

'You mean that you will pitch it,' said Diogenes

'Ok, we will pitch it, but first we need to be trained in how to do the pitching and I have arranged for an expert to do this and she should be here any time now,' explained Mordechai.

A flamboyant elderly lady was moving towards them in a rather irregular line that caused the other customers to hold onto their drinks to avoid her swaying movement. She recognised Mordechai and positioned herself in a direct line to his table before she kissed both of them and sat down. The waiter nodded towards her as if to say, the usual, and it was not long before the table was heaving with French fries and southern fried chicken alongside glasses of beer. In the middle of this she was examining Mordechai's material through thick glasses.

'Ok guys, I am Belulah, and I have spent all my life in or around movies. This stuff looks good to me, but I know that the producers ain't no dumbos. They get ideas thrown at them all the time and our job is to make this stand out. I would suggest that the two of you work together and then you have double the chance. So each one takes a different queue, making sure you don't duplicate, and then give out cards and stick to the same message.'

Belulah scribbled away until she had a summary of the main points on one side of a card.

'Remember that you have to get the producer hooked and he must be out of his mind wanting to know where your protagonists are going and what they want.'

'But it's not finished yet,' said Diogenes.

'That don't matter, you must remember that this is only the first stage. If the producer bites, there will be many more chances to think about that and the finished article may bear little resemblance to the book as you know it,' said Belulah.

'But what's the point of that?' protested Diogenes.

'Listen,' said Mordechai. 'The point is, that without some form of publication the project will be of limited value. I assume you want others to see it, and so this is a way of getting it into the public arena.'

'See what?' said Diogenes.

'Who is this guy?' said Belulah. 'Who cares what they see as long as they see something and the money comes in.'

Diogenes got the message and prepared himself for the next day's work whilst unconvinced, but at the same time, committed to the cause.

The following afternoon Mordechai and Diogenes were back in the bar with just drink on the table and hardly able to speak, after several hours pounding out the same message to producers who were trying their hardest to look interested.

After a night of single malt, Diogenes caught a flight to London, but it was the afternoon before he could gather the strength to catch up with Marie in the laboratory. She leapt out of her chair and pulled a bottle out of the crate of single malt, as she settled him into a swivel chair so that he could move about with ease.

'Glutamate, that's it,' announced Diogenes.

'Glutamate,' said Marie.

'Yeah, glutamate, that's where we're at. It's the key to these conundrums. It has been sitting in front of us all the time and we didn't see it. All these problems with brain washing and its detection and how to control the neurones, seem to involve glutamate.'

'But which part of the brain are we looking at here?'

'I think it varies but the insula and the anterior cingulate gyrus look promising, so we are getting nearer all the time,' said Diogenes.

'But how are we getting nearer?' asked Marie.

'Well I have a contact in California who is heavily into detecting glutamate as we speak, and if this works then we can link this to our ability to paralyse the bombers. It is important that we select who to use, otherwise we just paralyse everyone.'

'I see, so we are saying that high glutamate alone is not necessarily dangerous unless you link it with a bomb or a similar device,' said Marie.

'I think so. Can you think of any other high risk material?' asked Diogenes.

'Well I can, what about nerve gas, bacterial toxins or other materials?' said Marie.

'I hadn't thought of that. Do you think that's likely?'

'Maybe not yet,' said Marie.

Diogenes was in need of a top-up and he poured out some of Marie's golden nectar. Maybe the level of glutamate had to be so high that they could neutralise it without worrying what the bomber was going to do, or maybe the paralysis needed to be short-acting so they could act quickly. There was no way of testing this other than using human volunteers, and there was no better supply other than in Cyprus.

Diogenes's phone rang: "Hello it's Tamuz here. Look I've had the go-ahead from General La Rochelle and we have the clearance to move the luggage to the usual place, and we will embark at 03.00 hours continental time. See you there at lift off," he announced in code.

Diogenes turned to Marie.

'I think we are on for Cyprus, so get your case packed.'

26

Despite Miles's best efforts, the logistics of getting Carlo to the White House was proving impossible, so a compromise was reached where Miles met him in the VIP lounge in the airport and took possession of the box. A limo was laid on and Ingrid was waiting ready to put her patient on a heart-lung machine for the procedure. Fortunately, Freddie had provided instructions on cleaning out the debris before and then how to spread the glutamate paste along the spinal nerves and canal where it had been affected. It was then just about seeing whether she could wean the patient off the heart-lung machine. After a few irregular beats, and with the help of some electrical stimulation, the heart stabilised. There was a collective sigh of relief as she cleaned up the wound and then closed up the incision.

Miles had left a message to meet him in the Café Morocco, just half a mile from the White House, where fine dining was the norm. Miles was now middle-aged, with a taste in clothes inherited from his forbears, who had made their fortune in the slave states and had many acres of plantations. Wherever he went in Washington the best table was reserved, which was expected when one could trace lineage back to George Washington. It was at a fashion show that he met Ingrid and it was her style and looks that led to theirs being the society marriage of the year that featured in the top magazines. Like most of Ingrid's acquaintances Miles had become mesmerised by her charms, but when it became apparent that she had talent that was beyond anything he had encountered, he failed to adjust. After that, it was inevitable that they would move their separate ways.

'Was the package satisfactory?' asked Miles over the aperitif.

'It was everything I had hoped for, as usual,' said Ingrid.

'Are Freddie and yourself an item then?'

'We are colleagues, Miles. He does the science and I do the cutting.'

'Well, that is an interesting take on the matter,' said Miles.

The meal consisted of an elaborate sequence of mini-courses with ingredients as obscure as their French descriptions that would have amounted to a mouthful in most normal restaurants. Many of the courses were barely eaten by either of them and there was the impression that the establishment only existed to entertain business customers and showcase the wealth of the one paying the bill.

'What's on your mind, Ingrid,' said Miles.

'You could always tell when I was ruminating,' said Ingrid.

'Go on,' said Miles.

'How much do you know about my Egyptian position?' asked Ingrid.

'I know more than you think.'

'Well, we are acting as caretakers there, but linked to the southern states, the CSA.'

'And so?'

'Well, I wondered about the views of the US, and how we stand?' asked Ingrid.

'I can't really speak for the president, but I am on various committees in the senate and we are strategically aware of all the major international matters. The idea of the southern states going it alone, as per the pre-civil war times, is not so much of a bête noir, as you may think. You see, back in the eighteen sixties, we had a whole bunch of territories wanting to break away and indeed take over. At the same time we had no emancipation of the Afro-Americans, which clouded the issue. So, if you are planning to colonise the Middle East, it is only in line with the pre-civil war divisions,' explained Miles.

'So, what you are saying, Miles, is that the USA might turn a blind eye, or even condone and recognise the new territories,' said Ingrid.

'I couldn't possibly comment,' said Miles.

'Can I ask one more thing, Miles, although I know I am being a bit cheeky?'

'You have always been cheeky, dear, and the answer is yes, I will appraise the president.'

Carlo made his way from Dulles International Airport to Grand Central Station in New York and then took the subway to the Lower East Side. He was eating pasta with a small fat man who had a five o'clock shadow and very little hair. Carlo was a slim, muscular good-looking man with greying black hair. His family had emigrated from Palermo in the early nineteen hundreds and on passing through Ellis Island came to settle on Orchard street on the Lower East Side of Manhattan with many other immigrants. He had begun life as an enforcer and he had fought in the professional ring as a light-heavyweight under the name of Carlo the enforcer. He had been good enough to go all the way, but other considerations had taken over and he was one of those who earned more money for what he didn't do. He was fortunate to have this background as it guaranteed him a job and a pension, whereas if he were left to the mercy of the market forces, he would be another welfare claimant.

'Where you been Carlo?' asked Franco.

'Oh here and there, Franco. Any news of Uncle Tony?'

'Uncle Tony, yeah, Uncle Tony, didn't you hear, he

got rubbed out in Central Park.'

'Central Park, you don't say, I didn't know he was keen on flowers.'

'It was in the middle of the night,' said Franco.

'Look Franco, I need you to pass a message to the consigliere. Tell him that Carlo has some business for him, big business. He should contact me here in New York, he has my number. But tell him I am going to need soldiers, but with clean passports. That's important; capisco.'

Franco nodded, he was always nodding, that was his role in the organisation, take this here, pick up that there; he knew all that. He was around two hundred pounds and five feet two. He always wore a white suit, but it had shrunk and become threadbare and forensic examination would have revealed quite a few surprises.

Ingrid was back in the White House with her patient who was beginning to mobilise slowly. This was a sign that the damaged nerves were mending and that Freddie's concoction had done its job. An assistant entered the room with a note on a silver salver addressed to Ingrid. She opened the note and read the brief message.

"To dear Ingrid, the family cannot thank you enough for what you have done. It was over and beyond what we expected. We know that this will be thanks enough for you, as you are a rare breed, but Miles and Inge have spoken with me and I am fully behind you in all your endeavours.

With fond gratitude,

The president."

Carlo had returned to Grand Central Station, avoiding Central Park, and was enjoying some gelati when he was greeted by a slim swarthy gentleman with his hair slicked back over his bald patch and a pin-stripe suit. He was guided into a coffee bar minus his gelati which had been removed from his hand and deposited in a nearby bin.

'Littering is a misdemeanour in these parts, my friend,' explained the stranger.

Carlo found himself with a cappuccino and a consigliere in a small café off the main concourse.

'Carlo, it is good to meet you. I have heard a lot from the family about your work overseas, but we still have some worries,' said the stranger.

'You don't say,' said Carlo.

'I do say, my friend. You are using a lot of soldiers and we don't see much in the way of our traditional work with numbers, narcotics, booze, loansharking or racketeering.'

'I see what you mean, but this is a big market, getting bigger, and it is developing so we are concentrating on establishing ourselves as a legit means of controlling the population. At the moment they are not the same as us, they want designer clothes, electrical goods and women but we have to educate them,' said Carlo.

'Education, that's a new one my friend. You mean we are going to need a professor of Omerta who teaches the family not to say nothing to no-one.'

Carlo had been away too long and even when he was back home he had not operated at such a high level. He had to get a clear message across to get support from the family for a further expansion of the organisation. He also had to get out of New York in a vertical position rather than like Antonio Caponigro in the 1980s, who had been found in a garbage bag with $300 stuffed up his rectum as a tribute to his greed.

'Look I am only trying to boost the family's reputation by working with the new Confederate organisation, whilst helping ourselves to the pickings. If we don't do it then others will, so that will make us the first established group and it makes us legit in the eyes of the bosses. Soon we will take over the Middle East and they all got plenty of oil and cash, so it's win win win for us,' said Carlo.

'Middle East, I heard of the Lower East Side. So what do you want from us?' asked the stranger.

'Just your good wishes and your goodwill.'

The stranger drained the rest of the cappuccino from the cup and nodded and that was the best that Carlo could hope for.

Ingrid contacted Freddie at the same time that Carlo texted Bill and a signal for operation Olive Oil was given to mobilise the invasion force and it was passed onto General La Rochelle and the Egypt-based forces.

27

Diogenes received a text message: "URGENT. Meet me at the gift shop in the British Library at 11.00 hours."

Diogenes turned to Marie: 'I am going to delay this whilst I sort this problem out. So stay on alert until I come back about this.'

Leonardo spotted Diogenes and they moved towards the cafeteria upstairs past stacks of postage stamps worth millions. Leonardo wore a Crombie overcoat and a regimental tie with his pin-stripe suit and expressionless face. In the spy world this man was the real thing, and the scar beneath his right eye appeared to have been inflicted by a bullet that had ricocheted off his night sight. His voice was like velvet and would have been an asset to any public school choir.

'I have been sent to apprise you of the latest plans for your area,' whispered Leonardo.

'I thought as much. My most recent message mentions a General La Rochelle who is unknown to me,' said Diogenes.

'This will soon become common knowledge as the general is a key player in the operation,' said Leonardo.

'So the work with suicide bombers and IEDs. Is that to continue?' asked Diogenes.

'Yes, because that will be of use in all our missions, but we are working in synchrony with a new invasion force headed by the general and based in the Confederate states of America. They are controlling Egypt and, as we speak, will soon be in control of Syria,' pointed out Leonardo.

'So where does that leave our missions?' asked Diogenes.

'We always keep our cards close to our chest.

Officially, we are simply neutral observers, but the real prize here is Iran.'

'Will this force just carry on into Iran?' asked Diogenes.

Leonardo hesitated, and looked around him, as he produced a brown envelope from his breast pocket that he placed inside a brochure on Persian antiquities.

'The CSA may have already bitten off more than they can chew with Syria,' commented Leonardo.

'Do you mean that the USA are going to be unhappy about being dragged into this?' asked Diogenes.

'Oh no, on the contrary, the USA are happy to be able to be seen as having nothing to do with this, and would want to back the CSA going it alone, as they no longer have the financial or moral support for any of these enterprises.'

'So who really cares what the CSA does?' asked Diogenes.

'Russia and China, who have an interest in Iranian oil reserves, and want to control any Iranian nuclear development.'

'So, how can I help?' asked Diogenes.

'It's in the envelope, but it means that you go to Iran and Russia and China, so as to divert the CSA from Syria.'

'So we support the Sino-Russian occupation of Iran?'

'I couldn't possibly comment,' said Leonardo, as he disappeared into the elevator, as if he had spotted a snake.

He checked his BlackBerry and found a message from his literary agent requesting an urgent meeting in the usual place, and so he took a cab to the Nelson's Column pub where Mordechai was scribbling on manuscripts with his familiar green pen.

'Ah, I have been trying to contact you. Good news.

One of the directors from the San Diego meeting has expressed some interest in our project.'

'What does that mean, Mordechai?' asked Diogenes.

'Well. It's good, very good. We could be at the Oscars with the red carpets and all the razzamatazz.'

Diogenes looked much underwhelmed. Poor Mordechai lived for these opportunities; derived his pleasure from basking in the pleasure of others in the movie industry.

'By the way, are we any nearer an ending for the project?' asked Mordechai.

'You mean that the director is interested without even knowing how it is going to end?' asked Diogenes.

Mordechai looked a little flushed as it hit home to him how fickle the business was even though he was aware that the finished movie may bear little resemblance to Diogenes's work.

'Well not exactly, in any movie there will be a flavour of the book and you will get all the plaudits and more importantly the financial reward, so they do all the spade work and you reap a large share of the credit,' said Mordechai.

Diogenes looked at his BlackBerry, it was getting late and he had to catch up with Marie. He guessed that she would have left the laboratory and so he hailed a taxi to her apartment. She responded to the intercom outside to tell him to come up. As he entered her hallway he could see her naked on the bed. She beckoned him to join her which seemed to be the ideal solution for the tight band round the base of his skull following all the day's events. As he entered the bedroom he could see that there was a visitor.

'Hi, I hope you don't mind if Helene joins us,' said Marie.

Diogenes couldn't think of an appropriate response

to the invitation so he simply smiled and took his place in the bed. Helene was a tall, slender, but muscular blonde with pale skin and green eyes. She smiled and shuffled over as she caressed and kissed Diogenes. Marie took her place on the other side of Diogenes making him the meat in the sandwich. Both of them massaged his body, one starting from the top and the other from the legs. He took turns kissing and caressing their bodies as both of them had erect nipples. He then used his fingers on their clefts until he could feel the moistness. Helen was shaved and he could more easily see the results of his handiwork as she pulled him towards her whilst simultaneously opening her legs and caressing Marie's nipples. It didn't take long until he exploded into her and he was gently moved on top of Marie who had opened the way for him. This time Helene was kissing him to help Marie and Diogenes complete the act. With Diogenes satisfied they proceeded to play with each other's sex organs with him lying between them in a lake of bodily fluids.

'Well,' said Helene. 'Marie had told me a lot about you, but this has been something very special.'

Helene disappeared into the bathroom and after a short time emerged in what could be described as formal business attire.

'I hope we meet again soon,' she said, as she let herself out.

Diogenes switched into business mode.

'Marie, we have to change direction in our research, and our work with a cohort of brainwashed individuals is going to be put into the slow lane. In addition, I am going to need more direction with it so that I can bring it into the public arena sooner rather than later. So I am leaving for Geneva tomorrow to see Professor Bi and work through some receptor manipulation. So, I am sorry to cancel, but I promise that it won't be long before we are on full alert and making a difference.'

After the early morning Geneva shuttle he was in Professor Bi's laboratory talking glutamate receptors.

'How far have you gone with glutamate detection?' asked Diogenes.

'Quite a way; we have an optical sensor that can pick up the density, and the next step is to make it portable and readable by a lay person,' said Bi.

'Do we have a timescale on this?' asked Diogenes.

'Well thanks to your generous grants we have a large team and I am getting daily updates, so I think days rather than weeks,' said Bi.

Another Chinese man entered the laboratory.

'Ah, let me introduce Li. He is a government representative to the People's Republic of China. He is my boss and organises my funding,' said Bi.

Diogenes acknowledged the visitor who was small but stocky in an ill-fitting grey suit and a red tie.

'Have you had any contact from LA?' asked Diogenes.

'Yes I have, in fact it is through this collaboration that we have progressed to the level of developing the optical sensor and we are now moving towards making it small enough to be accepted easily on a hand-held device. The next phase would be to link it to one of the devices that you have already to neutralise threat and render the target safe.'

'I heard that you are linked to the Americans, and I know that you are moving into the Middle East,' said Li.

'We are the scientific operatives, as you know Li, but there are serious terror threats all over the globe and we are working to make life easier for the peace-loving population, who are in the majority but at risk from the minority,' said Bi.

'Well I am more concerned about the political

aspects as you know, but Syria and Iran are very much on our political agenda and we would be concerned if the West were to take control,' said Li.

'Well Mr Li, as you know both Professor Bi and myself are at the sharp end,' said Diogenes.

'So, you are powerful men indeed and even dangerous yourselves?' said Li.

'I suppose we could be, but we are always at the mercy of our funders and masters,' said Diogenes.

'Are your masters hoping to take over the Middle East?' asked Li.

'We are not involved at that level,' said Diogenes.

'Interesting; do you think people would be against my country being involved, hypothetically of course?' said Li.

'I couldn't possibly comment but the Middle East has been out of control for some time and I would think that China is certainly one country that could do a good job there,' said Diogenes.

Li bowed to them both and thanked them for their time. 'Rest assured, your support from the Chinese government is stronger than ever and I am pleased at the bridges you have built here with our international colleagues. This is something we prize more than anything in the new world.'

Diogenes received a text message from Leonardo, "Get the next plane to St Petersburg. There will be someone to meet you. I have emailed the details."

28

Tamuz Halevy had been sitting in the Café Morocco with a cappuccino in the centre of Damascus. Most of the other customers had bloodstains and soiled clothes from the latest ceasefire declared by the government. Tamuz always drank alone; everyone knew him, nobody supported him but equally, no-one threatened him. He and his kinfolk had been there for generations making a living and managing their affairs like the population that had only recently left being Bedouins and had swapped their camels for mopeds.

Tamuz was disturbed by a dark skinned, slender man in a ragged brown blanket who limped in and sat with him. His chest was rattling and he pointed to some clear liquor on the bar. Tamuz squinted at him and called the barman who brought over a bottle. Tamuz thrust some notes into the barman's hand and nodded to the visitor.

'I wondered when you would get here,' said Tamuz.

'I couldn't just leave you to face all this on your own,' said Mamser.

'You are in danger of developing a conscience,' said Tamuz.

'I hear big things about to happen here; maybe your dreams will come true,' said Mamser.

'Is there anything new down in the Holy Land?' asked Tamuz.

'It's not so holy these days; there is a smell of war in the air and this time we don't have much in the way of supporters. The US is broke, Europe is worse and Iran is looking worse than ever,' said Mamser.

There was a rumbling outside the café and people were scattering all over including some who dived into the café. Mamser hit the ground and curled up in a ball;

he was used to this from the Palestine era when he had been a member of the Stern gang blowing up Arabs and British soldiers, whilst his friends were chasing girls. He had come over from Poland as a small child to avoid persecution, but his parents stayed behind only to be loaded on a train for one of the camps. Mamser was thinking of becoming a doctor, and he was determined not to be captured by the Gestapo and so he spent his last days in Poland killing whoever came near him by the use of a garrotte, until he could stow away on a fishing boat heading for the Middle East. That was how he earned his nickname of Mamser Ha-erev or bastard of the night.

The sound of machine gun fire was in the distance, but it quickly became closer and in longer bursts. This time it was different from the Syrian army gunfire and the gunfire was aimed at the soldiers in uniform who were on the streets, rather than from them. There were three saloon cars, each of which had some men with suits, who were spraying machine gun fire from the windows, after which they threw out some leaflets.

They read: "To all Syrian military personnel. This is the first operation designed to wipe you all out. It is in your interest either to desert or to lay down your weapons and go back to your homes. Cosa Nostra, Syrian Branch".

When the noise stopped everyone moved outside the café to see heaps of bodies in Syrian army uniforms and other paramilitary men in camouflage jackets picking through them, removing arms and uniforms, and throwing them in a pick-up truck leaving the bodies for the locals. This was invasion CSA style, with a Mafioso hit followed by a Special Forces reconnaissance to gather any weapons and intelligence that might help the cause.

In Cairo, Freddie was on the phone to general La

Rochelle.

'Have you got everything in place, general?'

'Well we have the logistics organised and the president has given us the go ahead to mobilise Confederate forces ready for a full invasion. The only worry we have is the Russians and Chinese, who might choose to make this an opportunity to start World War Three,' said the general.

'I think we have this in hand, general,' said Freddie.

'I mean, we don't want to start World War Three in a god-awful place in the middle of nowhere, over a bunch of camels and some half-baked nuclear device up the road in Iran,' said the general.

'I don't think we will have too much resistance in Iran and we have a couple of useful friends who will smooth the way for us,' said Freddie.

'And what about the Israelis?' said the general.

'Leave them to me,' said Freddie.

The Drohobyczerrebbe's phone rang. The rebbe was deep in study of the Talmud, by candlelight, as he whispered to himself the various interpretations and weighed their meanings according to the ancient scholars.

'Hello, this is Freddie, a close friend of Ingrid, I was wondering whether we could meet somewhere.'

'Of course, of course, any time. Can you come to my house in Beersheba at 14.00?' said the rebbe.

'I will be there,' said Freddie.

Ingrid would have done it in person but she was on extended leave in Helsingborg to finalise the preparations for her mother's funeral. Normally she was cool and logical in her approach but she had been close to her mother and had been influenced by her to go into the medical profession. Her father was a playboy with obscure offbeat interests who never stayed in one place for too long. She travelled from

Cairo across to Denmark and was drinking coffee in the Café Morocco in the centre of Copenhagen, wrapped up in stylish furs from a Swedish elk. Inge had flown in from New York for the preparations, and their father was due in from Iceland any time. The Café Morocco could not have been more of a contrast to its Middle East namesakes. It was spotless, minimalist, and roomy and with an executive clientele who were there for the Turkish delight and oriental pastries.

'I have been reading about your adventures all over the globe, sister,' said Inge.

'I wouldn't call them adventures, Inge; just an honest girl doing an honest day's work,'

said Ingrid.

'I have been talking to Mr al-Aleppo; you remember him, yet another one who had his life saved by yourself. He is back to normal now, thanks to you, and wants to help in any way he can,' said Inge.

'And has he any views about the future of his country, Syria?' asked Ingrid.

'He said that he will not go back until Syria has become free and he will use his influence to support anyone who can help,' said Inge.

'Even the Confederate States of America?' asked Ingrid.

'Absolutely,' said Inge. 'Indeed, he has an offer that may be of some help here. He has suggested that you use Cyprus as a staging base.'

'But what of the north-south divide there and the Turkish-Greek hostilities? I thought they were at each other's throats,' said Ingrid.

'At the moment with the world in a financial meltdown nobody is too interested in wars and anyway, you could use Akrotiri which is a British-owned military base, so neither Turkey nor Greece could object,' said Inge.

'What does Mr al-Aleppo think?' asked Ingrid.

'He is all for it. He sees Syria as a country which is not fit for purpose and urgently in need of some guardianship and sound governance and he doesn't care who provides it,' said Inge.

'Have you told general La Rochelle about the prospect of using Cyprus as a staging base?' asked Ingrid.

'Just waiting for your go ahead, sis,' said Inge.

Their father joined them and the conversation became a mixture of cordialities and a list of his recent research findings. Inge and Ingrid had been brought up on this since childhood and had watched as their father introduced a string of attractive female research assistants who passed through their home. Their mother was a typical doctor with little time for anything as she stoically ignored the floozies and fed her children.

Freddie had flown over from Cairo and driven to a rather derelict stone house in Beersheba. It was not the sort of place that he was used to and he always felt that, because of his royal connections over the centuries, opulence was part of his DNA. He had to almost bend double to enter the open door of the Drohobyczerrebbe's house. He was rather unclear as to which direction to go in as he continued to stoop, as his eyes adjusted themselves to the dark. The room could have been a dining room or a bedroom, as it was difficult to see much of it, due to heaps of paper in a variety of languages. Some of them were in Hebrew, others were English and the rest were in Aramaic and other dead languages. The carpet was threadbare, and what could be seen of the walls was stained with scraps of old wallpaper. The rebbe was sitting on a throne-like armchair that would have failed a risk assessment in Western countries. The rebbe came from a line of scholars, going back to the eighteenth century in

Drohobycz, when it was part of the pale of settlement in the Austro-Hungarian Empire. The rebbe's job had changed little over the centuries, and most of his money came from the business of dealing in amulets, Holy Scriptures and being a spiritual adviser to those who sought help. Donations were always forthcoming either in cash, gold or food. Although more recently he was a Jewish resident of Israel, he did not see himself as a loyal citizen and, along with his followers, he had not done his national service or paid tax.

'How can I be of help Freddie?' said the rebbe.

'You will remember Ingrid from Cairo. She is becoming concerned about Syria and wants to help set the people free and she mentioned that you have some interest of your own in the area,' said Freddie.

'Indeed, I am much of the view that the Jews should be looking at Assyria or Syria, as it is now known, as their ancestral home rather than Israel, according to some ancient tracts that I have examined,' said the rebbe.

'The question is, how you can organise the Jews to move to Syria when the country is secure?' asked Freddie.

'Well Freddie, since the beginning of time the Jews have been looking for a land of their own that is secure. They thought that Israel would be the answer, but we all know how much of fool's gold that turned out to be,' said the rebbe.

'But how do you sell it to the Jewish people?' asked Freddie.

'That is easy, you don't need to bother,' said the rebbe.

'I don't understand,' said Freddie.

'If you look back over history the Jews have been invited into countries by various kings and emperors to help with their money problems. In return they have been given citizenship, and they were protected by the state. Those Jews who want peace and prosperity will go of their own free will and the others will take their chance and stay where they are, being bombarded by their Arab neighbours,' said the rebbe.

'But what about the law of return, where all Jews have the right to settle in Israel?' asked Freddie.

'But even that is not absolute, as criminals are denied the right, so Syria can also pick and choose which Jews they would allow in the country, like any other state,' said the rebbe.

The Drohobyczerrebbe called his aide to bring him lemon tea and kichel biscuits made in the Polish way and Freddie, having glanced in to where the food was kept, made an excuse and left, with a nod of his head.

29

Diogenes had bought a business suit at Geneva Airport prior to his flight to St Petersburg. He easily picked out the chauffeur with his name on a board as being the only one that appeared to be slim and clean. The black Mercedes was waiting outside the terminal building with a uniformed policeman next to it. There was no conversation as they manoeuvred around the pot-holed roads and broken-down Ladas. They parked outside a large palace with sentries outside and Diogenes was ushered into a waiting area with ornate ceilings decorated with battle scenes. There was a samovar and china cups with a carved wooden box full of teas.

Before long a large dark man in a suit beckoned Diogenes along a corridor and he opened a double door to yet another waiting room, but this time with a secretary at a desk who looked at him with a rictus grin. She appeared to be grooming her nails, out of either boredom, or in preparation for her night stint at one of the five-star hotels that supplemented her income with American dollars. Her phone buzzed and she stood to announce that Commissar Nevsky would see Diogenes.

The commissar's room was vast and it was difficult for Diogenes to focus on the commissar, as he poured some tea for his guest. As he turned round Diogenes strained to pick out his features, and as he spoke, he realised that the man was no other than Alexei, whose apartment he had visited and met the chickens.

'We meet again,' said the commissar.

'Indeed, you seem to have had a rather rapid promotion,' said Diogenes.

'Well, that is one way of looking at it. I am told that the UK government wishes us to have some preliminary discussion.'

'Yes, so I am told. It is about the Iran question,' said Diogenes.

'I see, does your government have any proposals or plans in the area that we should be aware of?'

'I wouldn't say that they have any plans, it is just that they are aware of the universal concern that we all share about this country and they wondered whether Russia had any thoughts about how to solve this conundrum,' announced Diogenes.

'As you know, Iran is our neighbour and, like the rest of our neighbours, we do have concerns about their welfare. The area has a long history of transition, some good and some not so good. At the moment things are not going so well for them and the religious and secular elements struggle to find a compromise. This was the case in your country in the past, but in many other countries it still happens and although they have a dictatorship, we in the East are more tolerant than yourselves of this situation,' said the commissar.

'But what of the nuclear threat?' asked Diogenes.

'I have heard that they are enriching uranium like all of you, but the process of moving forward from this enrichment to effective nuclear weapons is not so simple,' said the commissar.

'Are you saying that Russia is content to let its neighbour continue along this course?' asked Diogenes.

'We have many neighbours who do things with which we may not agree, including Syria, but that doesn't mean we will want to change them. It may not have been an easy transition for some of the countries and they have made their own mistakes, but we do not want to reverse this trend. I hope this answers your questions,' said the commissar.

Diogenes smiled weakly. This was not the Sergei that he remembered of old, but then Russia was a vast country in transition and he had seen for himself the polarisation of the population and how simple it was for thoughts to change. He nodded and was ushered back to his waiting limo to the airport.

The journey seemed smoother than before, without the human disorganisation on the roads, and before long he was ushered into another palace. This one was not as grand as the other one and he was asked to wait in a rather bare room with a uniformed officer in a chair by the door. There were no refreshments offered and any attempt at conversation was met by a cold stare. Another officer in uniform emerged from a room to ask him to sit at a desk and there was a plain clothed official next to him. This room had only the minimum of furniture, practical but not comfortable. The plain clothed official was smoking and had a dark grey suit of the type that looked government-issue.

'Who are you?' asked the official.

'I have been asked to visit by the UK government,' said Diogenes.

'You are a diplomat or are you a spy?' asked the official.

'I am a citizen and a scientist,' said Diogenes.

'A scientist, I see. You are a nuclear scientist?' asked the official.

'Why have you brought me here?' asked Diogenes ignoring the question.

'I am asking the questions.'

'I have diplomatic status and I am not under any obligations to answer any of them,' said Diogenes.

'We can keep you here for a long time and no-one would know,' the official reminded him.

Diogenes was moved to another room where he was given some tea and biscuits whilst he texted Marie and asked her to proceed with the Central American project and he arranged for the necessary visa and passes to get her on a flight from Brize Norton.

On disembarking she was met at the camp in the holding facility, by a British army captain, who directed her to the medical block.

'We have the clients here and they have been labelled and indeed tattooed appropriately ready for the work you need to do. I presume you are aware of the codes?' said the captain.

'Indeed I am but I just want to do a repeat Milgram experiment on them to double check,' said Marie.

'We have them in separate blocks as we thought you might need them to be isolated. What is the next step?' asked the captain.

Marie rigged up a chair and a desk for each prisoner with a dial that could be used to increase the frequency of electric shock. In the same room behind a screen they arranged for a volunteer sham victim for each shocker, who was instructed on how to simulate pain in increasing severity. An interpreter instructed the shockers on how it worked and the same man wearing a white coat would mingle with them giving vague signs of encouragement. The same experiment was rigged up separately for the other group in another part of the complex.

As expected the experiment showed that within normal limits the two groups could still be recognised by their polarised results. The next step was to take blood samples from each group to determine whether their glutamate levels were different and whether the levels were significant.

Diogenes received a text message from Leonardo. "Get back to London and contact me ASAP."

He texted Marie: "We need to move quickly, meet me at the lab."

Diogenes met up with Leonardo in Hyde Park by the Serpentine.

'Do you have the necessary equipment for any

incursions into foreign parts?' asked Leonardo.

Diogenes nodded.

'We have another rather worrying development in the area, which was not unexpected, given our recent discussions, in that Russia has begun to amass troops on their borders with Iran,' said Leonardo.

'Do you think they are planning to attack?' asked Diogenes.

'We can't be sure at this stage, they often announce practice manoeuvres when there are international tensions to warn off other interested parties,' said Leonardo.

'And what do we do?' asked Diogenes.

'I first want you to see a friend of mine tomorrow. He is one of our top men in uranium enrichment and nuclear fission.'

'And then?'

'He will train you in the rudiments of what it takes to be a nuclear scientist, in a day, and then I want you to go in to Iran,' said Leonardo.

'But won't they just kill me or take me as a hostage in Iran?' asked Diogenes.

'We have thought of that. You will meet up with one of our good friends, Mamser Ha-erev, and he will pass you off as a dissident Israeli nuclear scientist, who has a grudge against his homeland, and then you can mingle with the Iranian scientists,' said Leonardo.

'But why do they need another nuclear scientist, especially one with dubious credentials?' asked Diogenes.

'Because their own home-grown ones are being blown up at a rate of knots, probably by Israel, and a full-scale bombing of their facilities is imminent,' said Leonardo.

By this time they had done about ten rounds of the lake and they moved out of the park to the Café

Morocco. They sat on tubular bamboo chairs and ordered cappuccinos.

'You should also know that Syria is being invaded, as we speak, by the Confederate States of America, and they may be interested in Iran at some time,' said Leonardo.

'I spoke to a senior Chinese figure when I was in Geneva and I got the idea that they would welcome a regime change,' said Diogenes.

'Everyone is interested in Iran but only for the oil. Our interest is to prevent a war, particularly if there is a nuclear possibility,' said Leonardo.

'And what of the Arab League?'

'They sit on as many fences as they can find,' said Leonardo.

Diogenes returned to the lab where Marie was looking rather puzzled with a large tub postmarked Geneva on a bench nearby. Diogenes dashed over to the tub and wrenched it open to reveal smaller tubs, bottles, aerosols and other equipment with dials. There was a leaflet marked glutamate detection and diagrams, in between the equipment.

'He has delivered,' announced Diogenes. They both pulled all the contents from the tub and began to assemble it.

As Marie began to feel warm and amorous, Diogenes appeared more pre-occupied and distant. He received a text message: "All that you need is arriving by courier at 3pm."

'I am afraid I am off again very soon, dear,' said Diogenes.

'Am I coming with you?' asked Marie.

'Maybe tonight, but not after that,' joked Diogenes.

After collecting the parcel from the courier he paid a visit to Mordechai in his office.

'How did we get on in San Diego?' asked Diogenes.

'Let's say they were rather underwhelmed but too polite to tell us,' said Mordechai.

'So where next?' asked Diogenes.

'Well I haven't had anything more from you since last time. When do you think we are going to get to some closure here?' asked Mordechai.

'I think I will be in a position to round off the novel very soon, but I have to go away again and you might not see me again,' announced Diogenes.

'What do you mean?' asked Mordechai, looking quite devastated.

'Oh I don't mean that I am going to change agent, it's just that I can't really say much more at this time.'

Mordechai looked more relieved. 'Well I wish you all the best, and I promise that we will have everything ready for you, on your safe return.'

Diogenes landed at Teheran airport.

30

Tamuz Halevy was making his way down the street to pick up his tobacco, avoiding shrapnel and debris. The possibility of the Americans coming over to Syria was appealing and he saw himself as one of the few links with the past as there were hardly any others to take over the role.

As he made his way through the chaos he heard a loud noise and just a few metres in front of him, on the road, he saw the body of a soldier. There were no other bodies and there was no sign of blood or wounds. As he bent over the body he could see that the man was a senior officer, by the gold stars on his epaulettes. His hat was covered by gold oak leaves and his tunic had layers of medal ribbons above the left breast pocket. Tamuz looked down the street to see five men in traditional dress running down an alleyway. He glanced inside the Café Morocco but noticed that there were no other customers and the bartender was cowering at the back, with the rest of the place virtually unscarred, apart from the table near the street. Tamuz continued down the street with caution when two more explosions could be heard in the direction of the parliament building. His BlackBerry showed a text message: "5000 immigrants on their way overland. Can you find us accommodation around Damascus? We have cash. Drohobyczerrebbe."

Tamuz had arrived at the store to buy his tobacco only to find a heap of rubble and some youths and women, in traditional dress, looting the contents. Tamuz cleared away some of the masonry until he found some tobacco, and gave some money to one of the men he recognised as the owner who was sitting alone on a rock. With 5000 immigrants on the way with their relatively new form of the Jewish religion, would this fit in with Syrian Jews with their crafts and tradition? The Jews dressed like the other Syrians and were accepted as such, so that the concept of Jews being different and a threat, had not surfaced. As he traced his way back to his house he heard gunfire ahead, but this was not the sound of militiamen or an army, it was single shots that ricocheted from masonry. Tamuz took cover from the sniper fire but was helpless in the face of an assassin who was invisible. He could see that the invasion was going to cost the lives of many innocent civilians unless the sniper threat was controlled. He remembered Diogenes from the past with his BlackBerry and he fished out his own BlackBerry and texted him.

"Diogenes, were are having some sniper problems here in Damascus, is it possible for us to get hooked up to your anti-sniper apparatus?"

Diogenes was in a queue waiting to pass immigration in Tehran when the text came through.

"That can be arranged Tamuz, but you will need to get someone with the technical knowhow to operate the app," texted Diogenes.

"I'll come back to you," texted Tamuz.

By this time Tamuz had managed to manoeuvre himself back to his house; he had just about exhausted all the prayers that he knew in the process. He lived in a stone built residence which had somehow escaped the ravages of centuries of discord but it was in need of refurbishment. There was no paint on the woodwork and when you entered the small doorway there was a display of assorted frayed wallpapers that his ancestors had pasted on top of the previous ones. Tamuz rang Ingrid who was back in her apartment in Helsingborg. She was sipping coffee from her Royal Copenhagen cup with a Danish pastry by her side when her

BlackBerry rang.

'Hello Ingrid,' said Tamuz. 'We are having a sniper problem here and I was wondering if you had any thoughts.'

'You know, I don't really, but my associate Freddie may be able to help, I think you have his contact numbers,' said Ingrid.

Tamuz had not had any contact with Freddie and he wondered whether he was the man to act as a go-between for these boffins. He realised that his surname Halevy signified the duty of his Hebrew tribe in assisting the priests and perhaps this was the modern equivalent. He rang Freddie.

'Hello, I am Tamuz Halevy and I am in Damascus. Ingrid has asked me to contact you about a problem. Can we talk?'

'Ah yes, Ingrid has mentioned you. What is the problem?' said Freddie.

'To put it simply, snipers. It has become difficult for us to walk on the street as they are hitting us randomly, so I wondered whether you could liaise with a friend of mine, Diogenes?' said Tamuz.

'Diogenes. I have heard of his work. I would love to make contact with him, but I am not sure whether that would be ethical with the current situation over here. I don't know who his masters are and whether there may be a clash of interests,' said Freddie.

'I know him well from work we have done in the recent past, but I believe that the future lies not so much with the Middle East or Syria but more with the situation in Iran,' said Tamuz.

Freddie could see that everyone was thinking this way, and that the growing nuclear threat linked with the fact that Iran was enriching uranium to weapons-grade levels, was an emergency. The takeover of part of the Middle East on behalf of the Confederate States of

America was just one part in the control of the threat and if Diogenes was working from a different angle to the same end, it could well be beneficial to collude with him.

Diogenes contacted Leonardo for permission to liaise with Freddie and share some of his research efforts vis-à-vis anti-sniper mechanics. Leonardo contacted his political masters in Whitehall.

'I have been asked whether we can help the CSA axis in Syria to eradicate snipers using one of Diogenes's gadgets. What are your thoughts?' he asked.

'To what end?' asked the minister.

'I think that we both know that the Iran picture is of the greatest threat to all of us and we have the Russian front on the northern Iranian borders as well as an unknown Chinese threat to consider,' said Leonardo.

'I see. I think it makes sense to have a Western alliance, even if it is rather loose in view of the emerging urgent uranium difficulty,' said the minister.

'So the answer is, go ahead?'

'We haven't had this conversation,' said the minister.

Leonardo texted Diogenes to give him the green light for collaboration with Freddie and Diogenes called Freddie to discuss the way forward.

'Hello Freddie,' said Diogenes. 'I think we need to talk nanobiochemistry.'

'Fire away,' said Freddie.

'Interrupt me if you have a problem,' said Diogenes.

'OK,' said Freddie.

'Right, we are talking glutamate receptors here. We have found that the levels of excitability of these receptors in different parts of the central nervous system are the key to either controlling man's behaviour or indeed paralysing or killing him,' said

Diogenes.

'So glutamate in their receptor forms, as distinct from any other form. But I thought that they were all interdependent?' said Freddie.

'That's what we used to think, but we have developed a method using high energy waves to isolate them. So then we can both detect and even modify or delete them, depending on what we need to achieve,' said Diogenes.

'How do we do this?' asked Freddie.

'Simple, we use apps on BlackBerries,' said Diogenes.

'And for snipers?' asked Freddie.

'We use the glutamate in the hypothalamus in the brain which controls the conduction fibres in the heart or we could either switch the heart off or depolarise cells in the brain and the optic nerve. In this way the sniper could either drop dead or suddenly lose the ability to move and see. Both ways he would be neutralised as a sniper and we could use this on one or many snipers by adjusting the strength of the waves,' said Diogenes.

'Is there any special skill required to do this?' asked Freddie.

'The operative does need some training but as long as he is intelligent and determined there would not be a major problem,' said Diogenes.

'Thank you for that, Diogenes. I think I know who we can use. How can we get him trained?' asked Freddie.

'Well I am a little tied up at the moment so I suggest you contact Professor Bi in Geneva. I will clear it with him,' said Diogenes.

Bill Stickleback left for Cairo airport en route to Geneva, to commence training.

31

Diogenes landed at Teheran airport and as he stood amongst hordes of Arabs being hugged by their friends and relatives he had a feeling of being alone and watching all of this from somewhere near the ceiling, as though it was unreal. He had a business suit with a shirt and tie and stood out from the others and he wondered whether his choice of clothes had been wise. He need not have worried as a dark figure moved to his side and asked Diogenes to join him in the Café Morocco.

'I am pleased that you could make it,' said Mamser Ha-erev.

'I thought I recognised you, but how was it that I managed to get through customs so easily?' asked Diogenes, with a sigh of relief.

'We have fixed everything, including for you to meet a highly influential nuclear scientist who is working with us, and I have some briefing documents for you to read before the meeting,' said Mamser.

'Will I not be under suspicion as a Western scientist?' asked Diogenes.

'The way things are over here, everyone is under suspicion, but at the same time no-one is under suspicion. This is a country of great history with many discoveries, but this has been tempered by revolutions and invasions. At present Iran is in freefall and many know that if they are to develop, they need the help of outsiders, whatever the ruling parties believe, much like the rest of the Middle East,' said Mamser.

'So where do we have these meetings?' asked Diogenes.

'I have fixed up a room in your hotel. You should use this device which will act to mask any monitoring from a hidden camera or other bugs. We have perfected these in some Israeli prisons as part of the techniques that we use for information gathering,' said Mamser.

Diogenes flagged down a taxi which took him to the upmarket part of the city and a grand hotel that was a fusion between the ancient and the modern. Outside were two guards, one was wearing a tight Western suit with a bulge beneath his left armpit whilst the other wore traditional Arab robes with a thick leather belt and a large dagger strapped by his side. Diogenes knew that if there was to be any dispute about his business in the hotel, it would be these gentlemen with earpieces who would be involved. They smiled as they opened the doors to reveal an enormous marble lobby and a semi–circular check-in. Diogenes was worried that they may have detected the sweat on his brow and in his hair, but perhaps they would take this to be due to the humidity. The check-in staff were quite charming and keen to welcome him with his foreign currency, as they handed him the key card. He was on the twelfth floor, overlooking hundreds of office workers but with a minibar full of single malt and other tipples designed for non-Muslim visitors. The television seemed to be jammed on Al Jazeera English channel and any attempt to change it resulted in a large red cross and the words "not available, apply lobby". He opened his dossier and noticed that it was dual translation English/Chinese. The introduction was around the enrichment of uranium and then there were lists of scientists with some background on them, some of whom were Arabic and the others Chinese. Diogenes felt that he had been fortunate to have undergone some briefing in London insofar as he was now quite an able amateur nuclear scientist, but he wondered why they didn't just send a real nuclear scientist.

Diogenes was in unfamiliar territory, operating with

knowledge that had not been derived from his own efforts and he was about to be launched into one of the most hostile and unpredictable of broken states in the world. He could feel the tight band around the base of his skull and he knew that the concomitant nausea and facial pain was due to follow. He opened the minibar only to find that he had drunk everything resembling whisky and he rang reception for some single malt. Within minutes a bellboy was knocking on the door with a box of miniatures which Diogenes had to sift through for single malt.

'Sign here,' said the bellboy.

Diogenes pointed to the single malt and asked whether he could just have more of those, only to be met by a glazed look from the bellboy.

'You no want this?' he asked.

'I want more of this,' insisted Diogenes, as his voice began to tremble with frustration.

He opened one of the miniatures and downed it in one and signed before deciding that the best course would be to go down to reception in person. He returned with a full bottle of single malt which would cost the same as several crates of it in most Western countries.

When he woke in the morning he found that someone had ordered eggs, breads and a variety of fruits and nuts served with tea that was neatly placed on a table next to his briefing data. A glance at his watch told him that he was running late and as he rose from the bed he felt a little dizzy and his appetite was not helped by the smell of the food as he reached for a cigarette instead.

He found the meeting rooms on the second floor and the delegates were busy drinking tea and eating pastries as they mingled. Diogenes had been to conferences all over the world, but he usually turned up late to avoid a room full of people and he often felt the urge to escape. A bell went to signal that the meeting was about to begin and Diogenes had noted that he was number three on the list of speakers. The seating was laid out in the lecture theatre with headphones for simultaneous translation and he noticed a booth at the back where some translators wearing headphones were placed. Diogenes knew from previous meetings that the translation bore little resemblance to what the speaker had said, and although the translators certainly had language skills, few had any technical knowledge, so the more specialised the conference, the further from reality was the translation.

The speakers were mainly Arabic but there were also some Chinese and the main thrust of the topics was about uranium enrichment and its advantages and dangers. By the time Diogenes took to the podium several of the delegates were rather sleepy and some were audibly asleep. Diogenes presented a rather manufactured paper about international variations in enrichment which went down much the same as the others. The conference gave delegates a chance of a break from their laboratories and a sample of travel, luxury and any deviant activity that was available. Diogenes knew that the meeting, in his case, was simply to introduce him to the group of the movers and shakers in nuclear Iran.

At lunch Mamser sidled over to Diogenes who had recovered his appetite and was working his way through the rice with lamb and chicken, along with a few miniatures that he had smuggled into the restaurant.

'How did you get me into this group?' asked Diogenes.

'It was not too difficult; as you can see, there is a high level of confusion here and I could have brought half a dozen bogus nuclear scientists to give a talk and it would not be spotted,' said Mamser.

'But what have we achieved with this?' asked Diogenes.

'We have established your credibility at this level and you have a toe-in to the system,' said Mamser.

A delegate came over to them as they ate and asked if he could join them and Mamser nodded as the three of them helped themselves to the dates and fresh fruit.

'I'd like you to meet a good friend from overseas, she is called Ingrid,' said Mamser.

Diogenes nodded suspiciously, it was not that he did not trust Mamser, it was just that he was becoming involved with an unknown character who might demand things from him and involve him in decision making. What made it worse was that, apart from being a delegate, she was stunningly attractive.

'I have heard of your work, and I have been invited here to see whether we have any common ground,' said Ingrid.

Diogenes had a problem with attractive females; it was not that he did not adore them, it was that he lacked any social skills to charm them.

'Where do you stand with this Iranian question?' asked Mamser.

'Oh I am with you, we need to do something, it is just that we don't know what, at present, and I am hoping you can show us the way forward,' said Ingrid as she moved back into the main room.

Diogenes smiled and nodded again. 'I hope we can meet up again during the conference.'

Mamser moved Diogenes into a side room where there were a small number of Chinese and other delegates.

Mamser took the lead and introduced Diogenes to the Chinese people and another Western delegate.

'I thought we should meet separately to iron out some shared aspirations about the Iranian vision for nuclear enrichment. There certainly is some common ground between China and us and I have arranged this project starting with a key meeting tomorrow morning,' said Mamser.

Diogenes looked a little puzzled and he went back to his room expecting a good night's sleep, but Diogenes was not designed for these activities; he was a head-down and charge-ahead type of person and when he had made himself comfortable, it was the single malt and cigarettes that dominated his activity. There was a knock on the door and when he went up to the circular spy hole he noted a slender blonde in a business suit. He unlocked the door and the visitor introduced herself.

'Good to meet you again,' said Ingrid.

'I do remember you and I took the opportunity to Google you, so I have to say that your achievements are quite remarkable, can I get you a drink?' asked Diogenes.

'I think this could be a meeting of a mutual appreciation society,' said Ingrid as she made herself at home.

Ingrid had no need to hitch up her skirt and this was not lost on Diogenes, as he focussed on her hot-spots.

'I think we are booked to give some talks to some Chinese delegates tomorrow and I thought that we could collaborate so as to maximise the impact,' said Ingrid as she tossed back her blonde hair.

The television was still stuck at the English version of Al Jazeera and the content was mainly bombs and rocket launchers accompanied by paramilitaries with one hand showing a victory sign and the other firing off a rifle. Diogenes looked on it as an Arabic form of muzak and would normally just turn it off, but as he grabbed the remote control, he noticed a group of about thirty men dancing naked in a city street. Upon closer inspection he realised this was happening outside his hotel and he pulled back the curtain to see the live action. Ingrid looked puzzled as she joined him at the window watching the entertainment, and they could hear the loud singing as the group gyrated. It was at this time that they recognised the dancers as being the nuclear scientists from the meeting.

Their lovemaking was like no other as both of them climaxed in a mixture of ecstasy and hilarity.

'How did you do that?' asked Ingrid.

'How did I do what?' asked Diogenes.

32

Bill Stickleback was sitting with Professor Bi in his laboratory in Geneva. This was a new experience for a man who had been used to institutions and orders that had to be obeyed. His time at Eton demonstrated that his academic prowess was close to remedial level but when it came to games and the army cadet force, he joined in everything possible. His fees were paid by an anonymous donor from military circles and rumour had it that he was descended from a highly decorated jungle fighter who had inherited money from a Trust.

Bill fiddled with his BlackBerry whilst the professor patiently sat with him talking glutamate technology. Bill had a habit of blacking out matters that sounded complex.

The professor showed him how the new weapon could be linked to his BlackBerry that could be carried in his pocket and required the operation of a few buttons and Bill rapidly felt empowered. He called in some favours from a colleague who volunteered to parachute him into Syria, and before long he had rendezvoused with Tamuz in the Café Morocco.

The invasion of Syria was progressing to plan, which was surprising given the rather unorthodox army of Mafia, the SAS and a unique nanobiochemical device designed by Diogenes. As they progressed through the streets, the carnage was obvious with bloodstained bodies, wailing women and craters caused by aerial bombardment from the government. He could hear the sounds of bombers in the background and soon realised that the CSA had launched a full invasion from off the coast of Cyprus.

Bill received a message on his BlackBerry. "Our ambitions in Syria are going to be seriously compromised at this time so please lie low, Inge."

At this time Inge was in a United Nations meeting with his friend al-Aleppo and a high-ranking Russian official.

'We are aware of your ambitions in Syria and the president of Russia has asked me to make it clear to you that this is not acceptable,' said the Russian.

'There are many in my country who want another power to take over to reduce the civil war situation that is killing our civilians,' said al-Aleppo.

'We can see that, but what I am saying is that Syria is of great strategic importance to Russia, not only due to our bases but also due to our long ties of friendship and trade,' said the Russian.

'I think we need to look at the international situation. Syria is in a self-destruct mode and Iran is threatening the civilised world. The United Nations cannot stand idly by whilst this continues as it threatens world stability,' said Inge.

'We have no intention of letting another superpower take over one of our long-term allies,' said the Russian.

'It is happening as we speak,' said al-Aleppo.

'Then this is tantamount to war and we will act in an appropriate manner,' said the Russian.

Inge excused himself and visited an office down the corridor before returning with a Chinese delegate.

'May I introduce Professor Li from the People's Republic of China,' said Inge. 'Most of us now know that the question of Syria and Iran has taken centre stage in the affairs of world peace and there has been little progress at the level of the Security Council.'

The others nodded and it was obvious that there was at least some agreement between the parties.

'Ideally we would like these countries to be self-governing but they have proved to all of us that they are unable to maintain this status. Before we go any further can I suggest a compromise agreement that we can use to start discussions, before we go on to any details?' said Inge.

The others nodded and turned on their mobile phones for consultations with their respective governments.

EPILOGUE

Diogenes and Ingrid received simultaneous messages on their BlackBerries. "Urgent meet me at 2pm tomorrow in the Café Morocco in Oslo, formal dress, Leonardo."

Although travelling from different parts of the world they managed to share a taxi through the spotless wide Oslo roads and hardly noticed an explosion in the business area. By the time they had arrived Leonardo had secured a table amongst Norwegian troops in camouflage dress. Diogenes took out his BlackBerry and noticed that one of the apps had lit up. It directed him to confirm that one of the soldiers had a high reading. At this time an official entered the café ready to escort Diogenes and his colleagues to the Nobel Institute across the road.

'It works,' exclaimed Diogenes.

'What works?' asked Ingrid.

'Come on,' said Leonardo with a wry smile. 'We are due down the road.'

They entered the Nobel Institute through the main door.

The chairman of the Nobel committee opened the proceedings and read out the citations.

CITATION FOR DIOGENES, NOBEL LAUREATE.

The advent of nanoscience along with development in smartphone technology, have been one of the success stories of the twenty-first century. Along with this, the concept of manipulating brain receptors, especially in the form of glutamate, have revolutionised our understanding of human behaviour. However there has been a continuance of wars and atrocities committed by certain failed states against their own citizens. For the first time we have managed to harness scientific developments to enable atrocities to be neutralised to a degree that allows more civilised powers, who abide by the international rule of law, to take control and deliver stability. This novel concept would not have been possible without the laboratory developments that underpinned these new weapon systems that could minimise bloodshed in conventional warfare.

CITATION FOR INGRID KARLSSON, NOBEL LAUREATE.

Despite the many advances of modern medicine and surgery, there were many cases for whom if treatment had not developed they would simply become chronically damaged or deceased. We have developed systems for the transplant and replacement of organs, especially in the brain and central nervous system that can return full functioning. In this way the international medical community has acted as a leader, not only in their own field, but also in international relations.

ADDRESS BY THE NOBEL CHAIRMAN.

The greatest threat to world peace has been the nuclear threat of Iran and the civil strife in Syria. The United Nations and the Western and Arab states have striven to control this smouldering volcano with no success. It has been possible to reach an amicable arrangement where the state previously known as Syria becomes part of the Russian Federation, whereas the state previously known as Iran is now part of the People's Republic of China whereas the Confederate States of America will overlook other problem areas.

The damage to the Syrian infrastructure will be

repaired under a generous grant from the Confederate States of America, the People's Republic of China and Russia.

I have great pleasure in awarding the Nobel Prize for Peace to Diogenes and Ingrid Karlsson.

www.ingramcontent.com/pod-product-compliance
Lightning Source LLC
Chambersburg PA
CBHW031318280626
47169CB00019B/2138